TACTICAL TAKEOVER

BROTHERHOOD PROTECTORS COLORADO BOOK #4

ELLE JAMES

TWISTED PAGE INC

TACTICAL TAKEOVER

BROTHERHOOD PROTECTORS COLORADO
BOOK #4

New York Times & *USA Today*
Bestselling Author

ELLE JAMES

Dedicated to my assistants, Nora and Michelle for keeping up with me and doing all those things I don't have time for.
And to my editor Delilah Devlin for jumping on my stories at the last minute to polish them and make them shine.
And to my transcriber, Kelly, who takes my mumbling musings and makes sense out of them.
You all keep my head above water and I love you for it!
Elle James

CHAPTER 1

Sawyer Johnson folded his long, lean form into the airplane seat, his knees touching the back of the seat in front of him.

Rain splattered the window beside him, the clouds in Denver seeming to sit on the airport.

Passengers filed slowly past his row on their way to assigned seats. As one man stopped to attempt to shove an oversized suitcase into the overhead bin, everyone came to a standstill.

After a two-hour weather delay, the crew was eager to get the plane in the air and on its way to their final stop...Colorado Springs.

After three attempts to fit a fat suitcase into a narrow slot, the passenger pulled it free and forced everyone standing in the aisles to back up to the exit door in order to have the bag tagged and stored in the belly of the aircraft.

Once again, the line of people moved past him, filling the seats, with the flight attendant urging them to sit and stow their belongings beneath the seat in front of them. She added that the sooner they all were seated, the sooner boarding would be completed, and they'd be on their way.

After the aisles cleared, Sawyer eyed the empty seat beside him, hoping it would remain empty so that he could move over and let his left leg stretch out into the aisle. Rehab had returned most of its functionality, but long bouts of sitting with his leg bent caused his leg to stiffen.

The flight attendant moved from the rear to the front of the aircraft, counting souls. When she arrived at the front, she nodded toward the ground crew indicating they could close the hatch.

A shout sounded from the jet bridge. "Wait!"

The attendant stepped backward to let a woman with sandy-blond hair race on board.

As soon as the blonde was through the door, she slowed her pace, ran a hand over her hair and walked down the aisle with her chin up, daring anyone to say anything about her entrance.

The hatch closed, the attendant checked the lock and lifted the phone. "Ladies and gentlemen, welcome aboard. As soon as we're all seated, we'll be on our way."

The woman checked the numbers above the seats and finally stopped beside Sawyer's row. She struggled to fit her small suitcase into the overhead bin, and then started to slide into the space beside him. Before she sat, she stopped. "If you want the aisle, I don't mind switching." She spoke in a soft southern accent that reminded him of basket of deep-fried chicken and sweat-soaked glasses of iced tea.

"Are you sure?" he asked, pulling the latch up on the belt to release it.

"Positive." She smiled tightly. "I don't like flying, but it helps if I can see out the window as we take off and land."

Using his good arm, he pushed to his feet and stepped past her into the aisle.

The woman slid into the seat against the window, and Sawyer dropped into the seat beside her.

He had to loosen the seatbelt all the way in order to chase the other side of the buckle one-handed.

A flight attendant walked by at that time, reached down, connected the two ends of the buckle and smiled. She didn't say a word, just moved down the aisles closing overhead bins.

Heat burned up Sawyer's neck and into his cheeks. He didn't like it when people helped him. He had to figure out things for himself, including buckling his own seatbelt using his good hand.

"I feel bad that I'm the last person on the plane," the woman beside him murmured. "I hope I didn't hold us up too much."

"It's been a difficult day in the airports," Sawyer

3

commiserated. "I almost didn't get off the ground in Dallas because of the storms here in the Denver area."

"Exactly," the young woman said. "My flight from Atlanta was over two hours late and barely made it here in time for me to make this flight. I was supposed to have long layover before I boarded the flight for Colorado Springs. And then the pilot almost had to divert to another airport because of the weather over Denver. We went around twice before the ceiling lifted enough for us to land." She raised the window screen and stared out at the runway. "I hope it's clear enough for us to get off the ground."

"It should be. Going out is easier than coming in under limited visibility conditions," Sawyer explained.

Still staring out the window at the rain-soaked airport, the woman sighed. "I just need to get to Colorado Springs. The sooner the better." She turned to face him. "I'm sorry." She gave him a crooked grin. "You don't need to hear me complain."

"It's okay. You're only echoing my thoughts. I'm ready to be in Colorado Springs myself."

She cocked an eyebrow. "Business or pleasure?"

He lifted a shoulder and let it drop. "Both, I guess. The pleasure part of it is up for debate. I'm going to check out a potential job offer and subsequent move to the area. What about you?"

Her smile turned upside down. "I gave up a good

job in Savannah, Georgia, to come out here. I hope I don't regret it."

Sawyer studied the woman. "You don't sound pleased to be moving out here."

"I kind of had to. My brother landed out here at one of the ski resorts. He's been living here since late last fall."

Sawyer tipped his head toward the rainy window. "Not much skiing going on during the summer season."

She snorted. "True. And he's had entirely too much time on his hands."

He glanced her way. "Getting into trouble?"

She nodded, opened her mouth to say something and closed it when the plane rolled backward. Her hand came up to grip his, and her eyes widened.

Even though the woman's grip on his good hand was tight, Sawyer didn't try to disengage.

As the plane taxied out to the runway, his seat mate must have realized she was holding his hand, because she let go and grimaced. "I'm sorry. The landing coming into Denver shook me. I admit I'm not looking forward to this short stretch to Colorado Springs."

She clutched her hands together in her lap and laughed nervously. "I don't usually hold hands with strangers."

Sawyer was just glad she'd held on tight. He was glad. He could help allay her fears. "No worries." He held out his right hand. "Since we're already past the awkward stage of touching a stranger's hand, I'm Sawyer Johnson."

She took his hand. "Kinsley Brothers," she said. "And thank you for not being offended."

"How could I be offended by a nice-looking young woman holding my hand?" After a brief shake, he let go and returned his hand to his lap.

That brief exchange had sent little bursts of electricity running up his arm and into his chest. He'd never felt anything like it and wondered if it was a residual effect of having had half his body blown up by an improvised explosive device.

Since the electrical impulses had happened to his uninjured side, he wasn't sure it had anything to do with the damage done that had ended the life of his buddy and Sawyer's career as a Navy SEAL. She was pretty hot and totally desirable.

Too bad he wasn't in any shape to ask her out. Though he'd regained much of his physical strength, he had yet to recover mentally. Thus, his reluctance in accepting the job offer from Hank Patterson, the founder of Brotherhood Protectors.

"Thanks," Kinsley said. "I appreciate that you didn't take it the wrong way." Her eyes widened. "Oh, dear Lord. I'm not going to get you in trouble for that, am I? I mean, you're not married, are you?"

Sawyer snorted. "Been there, almost did that. Didn't work out. So, no, I'm not married."

"Whew." She brushed a hand across her forehead. "Well, for me anyway."

"And for me," he assured her.

Kinsley shook her head. "Wow, I'm opening my mouth and inserting both feet, aren't I?" She looked out the window as they lined up on the runway. "I tend to rattle on when I'm nervous or scared."

"It's okay to be nervous or scared when flying. I was always a little tense on takeoffs and landings. It got better with repetition, but I never completely got over it." He gave her a weak smile. "And I've been up hundreds of times."

"And it doesn't get better?" She glanced his way as she chewed on her bottom lip.

"Not really. I just learned to compensate…think about something else."

She laughed without humor. "Unfortunately, everything I have to think about at the moment has me nervous or scared."

"Moving to another state, starting a new job…I get it. Change can me unnerving."

Her hands twisted in her lap. "And I'm doing it to be closer to my brother. I'm afraid he's into something he shouldn't be."

"How so?"

The plane's jet engines revved, and the pilot let off the brakes. Starting slowly, at first, the aircraft rolled down the runway, picking up speed quickly. Rain pounded against the wings and windows.

Kinsley reached for the armrest, encountered his hand and gripped his fingers so tightly, Sawyer worried she'd cut off the circulation.

The nose of the plane tilted upward. In the next second, the craft left the ground and rose into the air.

When they encountered the sky's ceiling, the plane bounced and jolted as if the clouds they'd entered weren't fluffy puffs of spun sugar but more like hard speed bumps.

Sawyer wasn't sure how she did it, but Kinsley's grip tightened.

While gaining altitude, the plane tipped to the right, away from the mountains, making a wide turn to head south toward their destination.

They hadn't completely finished the turn when the plane encountered a wind shear and plunged a couple hundred feet in less than a second.

Women screamed, and men cursed. Loose items were slung around the interior of the cabin.

Kinsley let go of Sawyer's hand and hooked her arm through his, burying her face against his shoulder. "We're gonna die."

"No...we're not." Sawyer clamped her arm beneath his and let her burrow her face into his shoulder. "We're going to Colorado Springs, and we'll arrive safely."

The captain's voice came over the loudspeaker. "I'm sorry folks. We just got word from the Colorado Springs airport. They're getting hammered by a hailstorm right now, and the wind is pushing another front through in the next thirty minutes. We're circling Denver International Airport to land. The agents at the gate will work with you to get you onto the first flight out in the morning."

A collective groan sounded from the passengers.

Kinsley chewed on her bottom lip, her eyebrows forming a V in the middle of her forehead. "I need to get there as soon as possible."

Sawyer stared out the window at the heavy clouds. "You do realize it's only an hour and a half drive, don't you?"

She glanced his way. "Is that all?"

He nodded. "Look, I don't want to spend a night in Denver any more than you do. If there are any available, I'm going to rent a car and drive down tonight. You can ride with me if you like."

"For that matter," her eyes narrowed, "I could rent one myself."

"You could," he agreed. "If you were planning to rent a car when you arrived in Colorado Springs, you might as well do it here in Denver."

"Is that what you were going to do… rent a car in Colorado Springs?" she asked.

He shook his head. "Not actually. I had someone coming to pick me up at the airport to take me out to where I'll be staying temporarily."

"Then it doesn't make sense for you to rent the

car. I should, and you can ride with me. Unless you prefer to be in control." She cocked an eyebrow.

He held up his hands, grinning. "I don't need to be in control. But you should let me pay half."

"That won't be necessary," Kinsley said. "I will be keeping the rental for a while. I have it planned into my budget for this trip."

"I'd take you up on the offer, but I'm going further than Colorado Springs. I'm headed for Fool's Gold, on the other side of the mountains from the Springs."

"Wow, me too. I'm going first to Fool's Gold."

He frowned. "Why Fool's Gold?"

She nodded. "It'll be my jumping off point." She glanced at her watch. "I'll have to stay the night somewhere."

"Do you already have a room?"

She shook her head. "No. I figured I'd find one when I get there."

"I understand Fool's Gold is a small tourist town. I'm not sure how many hotels are out there. You might end up going back to Colorado Springs to find a decent place to stay the night."

"I'd really like to be in Fool's Gold tonight, if at all possible. I need to find my brother."

"You don't know where he is?"

As the plane landed, Kinsley turned off the airplane mode on her cellphone and brought up an image of a map with a blue dot in the center.

"I have an app on my phone that allows me to find

my brother's cellphone. The boy carries it with him everywhere." Her eyebrows descended. "At least, he used to carry it everywhere." She held up the map for him to see. "That blue dot is the last place the application found his phone." She drew in a shaky breath. "That was a week ago. I haven't heard from him since."

"Could he have lost his phone?"

She shrugged. "Maybe. But he would've found another way to contact me. He promised to check in with me every other day." She brought up her text messages and handed it to Sawyer. "This is the last message I got from my brother."

He glanced down at the words on the cellphone screen.

YOU KNOW *the group I told you about that I joined out here? I think I made a mistake. Only now that I'm in...I'm not quite sure how to get out.*

SAWYER'S HAND tightened on the cellphone. "That doesn't sound good."

Her lips pressed into a thin line. "Tell me about it. That's why I'm on this plane, headed to the mountains. I don't know where exactly he is, but I have to find him."

"Where are your parents? Do they know what's

happening? I assume they're still alive and would like to know what's going on."

She gave him a slight smile. "They're on a world cruise and aren't expected to return for another two months. I'd hate to bring them back, and I'm not sure I know how."

"So, you're on your way to the mountains to bring your brother back on your own?" Sawyer shook his head. "What if he's mixed up with one of the anarchists' groups? You're not..." He waved a hand.

Her brow rose. "A man?"

"No. I could be wrong, but you're not trained for combat, are you?"

She chewed on her bottom lip. "No. I'm not."

"Even if you were, you can't go charging into one of their camps, demanding anything. They might shoot first, rather than ask questions."

Her mouth screwed into a twist. "Great. Now you've got me more scared than I was to begin with. I thought I'd drive out there, tell Derek to get into the car and get the hell out of Dodge."

"It all depends on who he's hooked up with." Sawyer shrugged. "It could go the way you said."

"Or not," she whispered. "I don't know what else to do."

The plane rolled to a stop at the gate, and people stood to collect their bags from the overhead bins.

Sawyer rose from his seat and, with his good

hand, pulled her suitcase out of the overhead bin and set it in the seat he'd vacated.

"Thank you," she said with a smile.

His retrieved his backpack out of the overhead bin, looped it over his shoulder then stepped back to allow her to emerge into the aisle.

"So, are you riding with me to Fool's Gold?" Kinsley asked.

"Do you trust me?"

She glanced up at him, her eyes narrowing. Then a smile spread across her face. "Actually, I do."

He figured a lot had to do with the fact he had one bum arm. What man could molest a woman if he had one useless limb? Sawyer sighed. "I'm glad. I'll even drive if you want me to. It's no fun to drive in the dark, much less the rain."

Kinsley lifted her chin. "I'll drive. But you have to stay awake to keep me awake. I'm already tired as I've been up since four-thirty this morning to get to the airport for my flight out of Savannah."

"Deal. I'll stay awake. But we might want to stop for coffee on the way."

She grinned. "We can do that. I could use the caffeine, too."

With the jet bridge in place, the door to the aircraft opened, and the flight attendant moved back to allow people to exit the aircraft.

"I guess we just have to hit baggage claim and the rental car counter," Sawyer said.

"I only brought my carry-on," Kinsley said. "What about you?"

He tipped his head toward the backpack over his shoulder. "I have everything."

"Good. There might be a rush for the rental car counter. I'd like to get there as quickly as possible," Kinsley said.

"Let's do this." Sawyer followed Kinsley off the airplane, working the kinks out of his stiff leg. Once it was in motion, he had no trouble with it. He'd even gotten back into running before he'd left Maryland.

Kinsley set her carry-on bag on its wheels and hurried alongside Sawyer, following the signs to the rental car counters.

Fortunately, they found a company without a line that had an SUV that fit Kinsley's needs, considering she might be traipsing around the backcountry to find her brother and would need something that could get into places a car couldn't access.

Within twenty minutes of exiting the aircraft, Sawyer found himself seated in the passenger seat beside someone who'd been a perfect stranger before they'd boarded the airplane in Denver.

"You sure you're okay with me hitching a ride with you? I mean, we only just met."

She nodded. "I am. Besides, while you weren't looking, I snapped a photo of you and sent it to a friend back home." She grinned. "If I don't contact her when I get to my hotel by midnight, she's to contact the Colorado State Police and file a missing and endangered person report."

Sawyer laughed. "Good for you. That puts the onus on me to make sure you find a room before midnight."

"Damn right, it does." Then she focused her attention on the road leading out of the airport in the driving rain.

"If you don't mind, I'm going to call ahead to let my contacts know I won't be flying into Colorado Springs. That way they won't head all the way into the airport."

"Go for it. At least you have someone expecting you in Fool's Gold." Her pretty lips twisted. "Must be nice."

He hated that she was on her own for the task she'd taken on.

Pulling his cellphone out of his pocket, he dialed Jake Cogburn's number. He was the man Hank had connected him with for the job in Colorado. Hank led the team in Montana. Jake, or Cog, as Hank had referred to the man, was the lead over the Colorado division of the Brotherhood Protectors. He'd be Sawyer's boss.

Jake answered on the first ring. "Sawyer, I heard that your flight was canceled."

"Hopefully, you saw that before anyone headed for the airport in the Springs," Sawyer said.

"I'd only made it to Fool's Gold before RJ called

and let me know. I turned around and came back to the ranch. I figured you'd be calling with an update."

"That's right," Sawyer said. "Rather than wait for morning, I'll be driving in. Should be there in around two hours."

"Great. I'll be up to show you where you'll be staying."

"Thanks."

"See you soon. Be careful out there. This storm isn't supposed to let up for a while."

With his boss notified, Sawyer ended the call and focused his attention on the woman driving. She was feisty and had a good head on her shoulders. He liked a strong woman who was loyal to her family.

There had to be a way to help her find her brother.

CHAPTER 2

KINSLEY DROVE out of the airport, wondering if she'd lost her mind. She hadn't known Sawyer for more than an hour tops, and yet here she was at night...in a car...driving with a stranger.

The man could be a serial killer for all she knew. He could have lost the use of his arm while attacking his last victim.

Her heart fluttered, and her breath caught in her throat.

She blurted out, "If you don't mind me asking, what happened to your arm?" Immediately, she felt awful. He might not be a serial killer, and the injury had probably been traumatic, and here she was demanding answers.

"It's okay," he said, his deep baritone raising goosebumps of awareness across her skin. "I lost the use of it in a firefight against the Taliban. We were firing bullets. One of them jumped out from behind a wall holding a grenade. Score ten for us, two for the Taliban. Or rather two and a half. I was lucky enough to survive the explosion. Two of my friends weren't so lucky." He turned away from her, but his reflection was clear to see in the glass.

His face was gaunt, shadows beneath his eyes, his gaze, like his memories, far away in another moment in time.

"I'm sorry about your friends," she whispered. "I can't say that I know what you're going through. I've never lost anyone close to me. And I'm not going to start now." Her hands tightened on the steering wheel. She'd set off on this journey with every intention of coming back with her brother. Alive.

Sawyer clasped his bad upper arm with his good hand. "My...disability..." he spoke the word *disability* with a harsher tone, "is part of the reason I'm going to Fool's Gold. You see, I'm no longer of any use in my former job as a Navy SEAL. But my new boss, should I accept the position, thinks I'm still viable. In a sense, I'm being given a second chance." He snorted softly. "Lord knows I need it. Not many people want to hire a one-armed former SEAL. Hell, I can't even hold a rifle against my shoulder."

She glanced his way. "Surely there are lots of things you can do that don't require you to hold a rifle anymore."

"I'm sure there are." He shot her a grim smile. "I've

never done anything behind a desk. Everything on my resume is about combat training, shooting, infiltration, extraction, explosives…you name it. I'm not trained for anything else." His lips twisted. "I'm not whining. I'm just speaking the truth. After I spent a couple months in rehab, I was trying to find a way to reinvent myself. I started some online courses, working toward a Bachelor of Science degree in business management. Problem with that is my stinking resume. Who will hire someone in management who has no experience in management? Then I got a call from an old friend—a Navy SEAL I'd fought alongside several years ago. I'm not even sure what my job will entail, but I'm glad to have the opportunity." He shrugged. "That's the short version of my story. What's yours?"

Kinsley hesitated. "My life has been boring compared to yours."

"We have almost two hours to kill. Try me."

His smile encouraging her, Kinsley tried to make her story sound interesting. "I grew up in a Savannah, Georgia with my parents and my little brother. I was the typical good girl, making good grades through high school and into college. I graduated with a biology degree and went on to get my Masters and Physician Assistant certification."

"So, you're like a doctor?" he asked.

She shook her head. "No. Not a doctor, but I am a healthcare provider. I can see patients and prescribe medications, but I have to work under a doctor's supervision."

Sawyer's brows rose. "That's impressive. And ironic. While I was out killing people, you were saving people."

"That's about as opposite as you can get." Kinsley smiled toward him. "I've always heard that opposites attract."

"Yeah, but even opposites have to have some things in common." He didn't meet her brief glance. Instead, he stared at the road in front of the car, his mouth pressed into a thin line. His hand remained clasped on his bad arm…as if reminding himself that he wasn't whole.

Kinsley frowned. "I bet we have more in common than you think."

"Like what?" He shot a glance her way. "Have you ever shot a man?"

"I've shot many men." She grinned. "As in *vaccinated* them with shots."

He snorted.

Kinsley held up one hand. "Okay, so that doesn't count. Besides, I'm in the business of saving lives, not taking them." She frowned. "But if someone threatens my brother's life, and it's them or Derek…I might take that kind of shot."

"Wouldn't that be going against the Hippocratic oath or something?"

"No." She lifted her chin. "Don't ask me why, but

it doesn't. Derek is the only brother I have. I'd like to keep him intact into our old age." She turned toward him briefly. "What about you? Any siblings?"

"An entire team of brothers," he answered, again looking straight ahead, his lips pressed together.

"As in your SEAL team?" she asked.

He nodded. "I have a sister by blood who lives with her husband in Galveston, Texas. But I rarely talk to her. She's busy with her own life and three little boys." His stern face softened. "She did come to see me when they brought me back to Walter Reed Hospital. I think her mother-in-law stayed with her boys for the week she was there."

"That's a lot for a mother to leave her small children for that long."

"She has a good relationship with her mother-in-law. They live in the same town."

"So, are you from Galveston?" Kinsley asked.

"I grew up just outside of Houston in a place called League City. We spent a lot of time fishing in the canals and swimming on the beaches in Galveston."

"Is that what drew you to the Navy and the SEALs?"

He nodded. "My father retired from the Navy and went home to Texas. He worked at NASA the last years of his life."

"You lost him?"

He nodded. "He and my mother liked to vacation

in Colorado. Dad had a skiing accident, which caused him to get a DVT. He didn't think much of the injury and didn't have it checked. Three days after he got home, he died of a pulmonary embolism. Mom died of a broken heart less than a year later."

Kinsley's heart squeezed hard in her chest. "That's so sad. I'm sorry for your loss."

"I was, too. I was on a mission when Dad passed. I didn't get home until after his funeral. Fortunately, Mom had a celebration of life for him when I was available to come. I was with Mom when she passed. I'd taken off the last two weeks of her life. Long enough to watch her fade way."

"That must've been hard."

"It was. But I had closure with my mother. I had a chance to talk to her, to tell her I loved her. To see her one last time. I didn't get that with Dad."

Kinsley's eyes filled with tears. She blinked to clear them. There was enough water on the road. She didn't need more inside the car. "Now, you're making me worry about my folks off on their cruise around the world."

"I'm sorry. And we're back to talking about me and depressing subjects. Maybe we should talk about what else we have in common," he said with a smile. "Are you a fan of football?"

She grinned. "I am."

"Favorite team?"

"That's easy…on the college level, the Georgia

Bulldogs. NFL, the Atlanta Falcons and the Washington Seahawks."

Sawyer sighed. "We're definitely on different paths."

"Why?" she asked. "You like football, don't you? I assume so, or you wouldn't have started there? So, who do you follow?"

"College level...the Longhorns and the Aggies. And the Cowboys for the NFL. Though I do follow the Broncos. Which is good, since I'll be working in Colorado. I'm impressed you keep up with the game."

"My father got me interested. I think he wanted me to be a boy. He taught me how to throw a baseball and to fish. When my brother came along, all three of us would fish. Eventually, sports became a father and son event. I wasn't allowed to play the team sports the guys played. Derek grew up playing baseball, soccer and basketball. I was proud of my brother's accomplishments but jealous of him at the same time. The only time we could be somewhat competitive was on the ski slopes. But then he got so much better than I was." She grimaced. "I have a fear of speed. It slows me down. I wasn't surprised when he opted to come out to Colorado to live and work at a ski resort rather than going to college."

"And you, being the older, practical sister, went on to college and then to get your Physician Assistant certification."

She smiled. "Boring, right?"

"But you've got a marketable career and a future in the medical field."

"And my brother came out to Colorado to have fun." Kinsley sighed.

Sawyer chuckled. "Do I detect a little more envy?"

"When I was knee-deep studying for the certification exam, maybe I was a little envious, but I'm proud of what I've accomplished. And I'm happy that I get to work with people, helping them to live better, healthier lives."

"You should be proud. You don't have to worry about getting a job. There's always a need for good medical personnel everywhere."

She tapped her palm on the steering wheel. "Exactly. Meanwhile, my parents are on a cruise ship somewhere near Singapore, I think. And I quit my job to come out to Colorado to keep an eye on my brother."

"That's giving up a lot for your sibling."

She shrugged. "To tell the truth, I've always wanted to live in the mountains."

"Not on the coast of Georgia?"

Kinsley shook her head. "Too hot, too humid and way too flat. I love the Rockies. They're amazing."

They talked from Denver all the way to Colorado Springs. The traffic was light at that time of night, and the rain kept even more people from venturing out. Once they made it to the Springs, the GPS map on Kinsley's phone had them turning west, leaving the city, and climbing up a winding road which led through a mountain pass.

The rain only slacked up a little. Still, Kinsley slowed on the slick roads, taking longer than they should have. She didn't regret it. Too often, she hit slick spots and hydroplaned in the unfamiliar rental.

The curvy roads were bad enough without the added pucker factor of slippery pavement. At one point, Kinsley hydroplaned and skidded toward a rocky escarpment. She was able to correct her course in time, but her knuckles turned white from how tightly she held onto the steering wheel.

"Anytime you want me to take over, just let me know," Sawyer murmured from the passenger seat, having fallen silent during the climb through the pass.

"Even if I wanted to let you drive, there's nowhere to pull off the road. Sorry, you're stuck with me behind the wheel until we get to the other side."

He chuckled. "You're doing great. If you want to slow to a snail's pace, do it. I'm not in a hurry."

She forced a laugh, though she was too nervous to feel the humor. She leaned close to the steering wheel and squinted at the rain-drenched windshield as if being closer to it would make it easier to see into the dark, stormy night.

When she finally emerged from the pass, Kinsley's arms ached with the effort of keeping the vehicle from crashing into a mountain or falling off a cliff.

"Are you okay?" Sawyer asked as the SUV rolled into the tourist town of Fool's Gold.

Kinsley let go of a long shaky breath. "I am now." She took one hand off the steering wheel and shook blood back into her fingers.

"Do you want me to take it the rest of the way out to Lost Valley Ranch?" he asked.

For a moment, Kinsley considered taking him up on it. But that would require stopping and switching drivers. "No. I'll be okay. Besides, we're really close now. It won't take much longer for me to get you to where you'll be staying."

"Yeah, but it would give you a break since you'll be coming right back to town to find a room for the night."

She shrugged. "I'll be okay. I'm just ready to get there and off the road for what's left of the rest of the night."

"I bet you are. I wish you'd let me drive that last stretch. It was a bear."

"I wish I'd known it would be that bad." She pushed her hair back from her face and slowed to take the left turn onto the road leading out to the ranch where she'd drop Sawyer. Her map indicated just a few more miles, and she'd leave him with his new boss. She'd head back to Fool's Gold to find a hotel she could base out of while she searched for her brother.

After spending the past couple of hours with

Sawyer, she wasn't looking forward to saying good-bye. He'd made her feel like she wasn't completely alone in Colorado. "Thanks for riding with me."

"Are you kidding? Thanks for letting me ride with you. The trip seemed to fly by." He grinned. "Unlike the plane."

She smiled. "Ha, ha."

"Liked that pun, did you?" He was still smiling as they drove past a busy little bar named Gunny's Watering Hole and pulled through the gate of the Lost Valley Ranch minutes later.

The man had a nice smile. His injury and inability to use his left arm had taken their toll on his confidence, but he hadn't lost his sense of humor.

Kinsley admired that in a man. In time, he'd learn to compensate for the loss of use of his limb. She really hoped the Brotherhood Protectors would be the right fit for him to rebuild his life.

The ranch's lodge was a two-story building with wrap-around porches on both levels. Lights glowed from the front door and all corners. A string of lights lit a path through the trees back toward the bar they'd passed on the way in.

It was a homey lodge that made her want to go inside, sit in front of a fireplace and drink hot cocoa.

As she parked in front of the building, a man and woman came out on the porch. The man walked with a slight limp. As the woman came to stand beside him, he slipped his arm around her waist and smiled as Sawyer opened the door of the SUV.

"Kinsley, I'd like you to meet Jake. He might have some suggestions for places to stay while you're in Fool's Gold. And I bet there's a pot of coffee somewhere inside."

Kinsley chewed on her bottom lip. "I really should be getting back to town."

"Jake could call around and secure a room so you don't have to hunt one down." Sawyer held out his hand. "I'd like to know you have a place to go before you leave me. I feel like we're friends. And friends look out for each other."

She stared at him for a moment, warmth spreading through her. "Thank you. I'd like that. But then, I really need to get somewhere so I don't have to drive again for the rest of the night. Tomorrow is a new day, but I'm bone-tired tonight."

"Deal." Sawyer got out of the SUV, hurried around the front of the vehicle and opened the door for her. He held out his right hand and helped her down from her seat.

As soon as Kinsley's fingers touched his, a shock of electricity raced up her arm and spread throughout her body, heat coiling low in her belly. She pulled her hand free and faced the porch and the two strangers coming down the steps toward them.

"Sawyer Johnson?" the tall man asked as they four met between the SUV and the porch.

Sawyer nodded. "That would be me. And you must be Jake Cogburn. Or should I call you Cog?"

"Jake or Cog. I'll answer to either," the other man said.

They shook hands, and then Jake turned toward Kinsley. "And who is this lovely lady?"

Sawyer touched Kinsley's arm, bringing her forward. "This is the angel who came to my rescue on the airplane that was supposed to bring us to Colorado Springs. Since we were both headed this way, she offered to bring me in her rental car." He smiled at Kinsley with such warmth it made Kinsley's knees weak. "This is Kinsley Brothers. She's moving out to Colorado and needs a place to stay for tonight."

Jake took her hand in his. "Thank you for rescuing my new recruit, Ms. Brothers."

"Call me Kinsley," she said.

Jake nodded. "Kinsley, I'd like you to meet my fiancée, RJ Tate. Her and her father own this ranch."

RJ gripped Kinsley's hand in a firm hold. "I'm glad you two made it here safely. That was quite a storm you drove through. They had golf-ball-sized hail in Colorado Springs. Did you run into any of that on your way in?"

Kinsley shook her head. "No, but it rained buckets through the pass."

"Well, it's about time you showed up," said a booming voice from the front porch.

Everyone turned to the barrel-chested man with a gray crew cut and a chiseled face, standing at the top of the stairs.

RJ shook her head. "Don't be so bristly, Gunny. These two have been through hell, tonight."

Gunny's eyes narrowed. "The pass was pretty bad, huh?"

Kinsley nodded, not sure yet how to take the man with the booming voice.

"Kinsley and Sawyer, this is my father, Dan Tate. In case you wondered, he's a former Marine Gunnery Sergeant. Thus, the loud voice that carries across the mountains and scares small children."

"Don't mind my daughter and her sassy mouth. She came by it honestly. Call me Gunny. I don't answer to anything else." He lifted his chin. "Well, don't just stand there, come in."

Kinsley hesitated. "I really should be headed back to Fool's Gold. I still have to find a place to stay for the night."

"You've come to the right place," Gunny said. "We have rooms here at the lodge. You can stay here as long as you like."

Kinsley blinked. "Are you sure? I don't have reservations."

RJ gave her a reassuring smile. "You don't need them. This is the offseason. Between the time when kids go back to school and ski season begins, we usually have openings. We'd be happy to have you stay. Unless you had prior plans to meet up with someone in Fool's Gold..." RJ cocked an eyebrow, waiting for her response.

"No. I really didn't have much of a plan at all." Kinsley glanced up at the lodge. "If you're sure..." Relief flooded through her.

As if to move things along, fat raindrops pelted the four standing in front of the house.

RJ and Jake ran for the porch.

Sawyer grabbed Kinsley's hand and ran with her up the steps, coming to a stop beneath the porch awning.

Gunny held the door for the four entering the lodge.

As Kinsley entered, she drank in the tall ceilings, the sweeping staircase and the massive fireplace in a great room filled with overstuffed leather sofas and chairs. The lighting was low, but enough to make a person feel welcome to sit and visit with anyone who happened to be sitting there.

At once, Kinsley was filled with a sense of warmth and homecoming. "It's beautiful."

RJ smiled. "It wasn't so beautiful when Gunny bought it. Back then, I thought he was out of his mind."

"Nothing a little elbow grease and determination couldn't fix," Gunny said.

The gunnery sergeant's daughter snorted. "Make that a lot of elbow grease and determination." She hooked her arm through her father's elbow. "But it's ours, and it looks amazing compared to when we first walked in. We worked one room at a time, bringing it back to its original glory."

"Was it always a lodge?" Kinsley asked.

Gunny nodded. "Yes, ma'am. It was built back in the late 1800s as an escape for the rich people in Denver. They would plan vacations in the mountains and come all the way out here to get away during the summer months. The last owner didn't use it to its full potential. He let it fall into disrepair. Business died off, and people quit coming. After the old man died, his heirs sold the place, as is."

"That's when Gunny made his shrewd investment, and we've nearly gone bankrupt several times over the past ten years." RJ chuckled. "Then Hank Patterson decided it would make a great base location for his venture."

"So, the Brotherhood Protectors is based out of the ranch?" Sawyer asked.

Jake nodded. "We have the basement and several of the rooms in the lodge for new hires until they find digs of their own. You'll be staying here until you decide where you want to live. You might like it in Fool's Gold or Colorado Springs. It's only a thirty-minute drive to the Springs from here."

"What exactly will I be doing?" Sawyer asked. "That might have a bearing on where I live."

"We do whatever needs to be done. You might act

as a bodyguard to someone in danger, rescue damsels in distress or extract someone who has been taken against his or her will. We do whatever needs to be done in situations the local law enforcement and government authorities might not have the authority or staffing to get involved in. Sometimes, we assist those agencies when additional, highly trained bodies are needed. We might also perform missions outside the US. Missions, similar to those we performed in Special Forces operations."

Sawyer's eyes widened. "Seriously?"

Jake nodded. "That's why we want the best of the best."

Sawyer's brow furrowed. "Then why did you contact me? You need able-bodied men." His hand once again clasped his limp arm.

Kinsley's heart tugged at the gesture that was becoming familiar the more she was with the former Navy SEAL.

Jake reached down and lifted his pant leg, displaying a prosthetic leg. "We might not be as fit as we were when we graduated from BUD/S, but we're mentally fit and find ways to compensate for whatever life has thrown our way." The former SEAL lifted his chin. "Believe me, I was where you are now —no, I was drinking myself into a bottomless pit of self-pity when Hank sent his guy Kujo out here to Colorado to recruit me into the Brotherhood Protectors. I didn't think I had what it took to do the job." He glanced down at RJ. "I proved myself wrong."

She wrapped her arm around his waist and leaned into him. "Yes, you did." She turned to Sawyer. "And so will you."

"If you're willing to take the challenge," Jake added. "Do you want the job?"

Kinsley held her breath.

Sawyer stared at Jake, meeting his gaze and holding it. "Yes. I do. At this point in my life, I have nothing left to lose."

"Except a shitty attitude about yourself." Jake stuck out his hand. "Welcome to the Brotherhood Protectors."

She wasn't sure why, but Kinsley felt proud of this man who'd somehow become important to her over the course of the two-hour drive from Denver.

"I'll take the job on one condition," Sawyer interjected, his hand still in Jake's firm grip.

Jake's lips quirked upward. "And what's that?"

"That my first assignment is to help this damsel in distress." He tipped his head toward Kinsley.

Kinsley gasped. "I'm not a damsel in distress," she insisted.

"No, but your brother could be in trouble, and you need help finding him." Sawyer released Jake's hand. "Kinsley's brother might be involved with a survivalist or anarchists' group somewhere up in these mountains. She needs help finding and extracting him from whatever group he's gotten tangled up with."

Jake nodded. "Sounds like something right up our alley."

Kinsley held up her hands. "I don't have the kind of money it takes to hire an organization like yours."

Jake grinned. "That's the beauty of the Brotherhood Protectors. Hank and his wife fund it. They want to help anyone who needs the help, regardless of whether they can afford to pay or not. Granted, some of their customers can afford to pay a lot. Others, might not be able to."

RJ raised a hand. "Like me. I was Jake's first assignment. Hank wouldn't let me pay him, even if I'd had the money to do so." She smiled up at Jake. "Jake kept me alive when I thought all was lost."

"We kept each other alive," Jake corrected. "The point is, we still have fight left in us. It's not time for us to be put out to pasture. We're needed."

"Thanks," Sawyer said. "I'll work hard to prove you right."

"Work hard to prove yourself right," Jake said. He turned to Kinsley. "Let's get some hot cocoa and show you two to your rooms. We'll get started on your case first thing in the morning."

Tears filled Kinsley's eyes. "Thank you. I'll find a way to repay the Brotherhood. I just need to find my brother. I'm afraid for him."

"We'll find him," Jake said.

A huge weight lifted off Kinsley's shoulders. After driving through the storm on the treacherous road through the pass and worrying about her brother, she had some relief. She had a place to stay, and she wasn't alone in her quest to find Derek.

CHAPTER 3

SAWYER WASN'T sure how helpful he'd be in Kinsley's search for her bother. However, knowing he didn't have to leave her to do it by herself made him breathe a sigh of relief.

"Don't worry," Jake said. "Hank's got a computer guy who can tap into just about any database in the world. If there's information to be had, he will find it. And we have connections with the local sheriff's department, and the Colorado State Police, that we can engage. Sawyer will stick with you to keep you safe in your search, but we'll be working behind the scenes to feed you information. And if you get in a tight spot, we can call in reinforcements. We can work as a team, just like we did on our special operations."

Sawyer drew in a deep breath, his chest swelling

with hope. "I like the way the Brotherhood Protectors sound."

"When I came on board, it was strange at first," Jake said. "Now, it feels like home."

"Speaking of home..." RJ reached out and touched Kinsley's arm. "Let me show you to your room. I'm sure you're exhausted and would like to hit the shower."

"I am tired." Kinsley glanced in Sawyer's direction.

"I'm not going anywhere," Sawyer said, as if in answer to her unspoken question. "You're my first assignment. "I'm going to stick to you like duct tape."

Kinsley chuckled. "Don't you mean like glue?"

"Glue doesn't always work that great on skin. In my experience, duct tape works better." He winked.

"I want to start my search first thing in the morning," she said.

Sawyer nodded. "I'll be up before dawn."

"Okay, maybe not that early. But, yes, I want to get going as soon as possible."

He gave her a mock salute. "Yes, ma'am."

RJ led Kinsley up the stairs, speaking softly about the lodge and what was available to the guests.

"Come on," Jake said. "Let me show you the headquarters of the Colorado division of Brotherhood Protectors."

"You mean the lodge, right?"

Jake laughed. "Not all of the lodge. It's still a

working dude ranch. People come to vacation here. RJ and Gunny offer trail rides on horseback and four-wheelers. There are old mine shafts on the property, and they have access to national forest lands where there are abandoned mining towns dating back to the 1800s. They also offer the ability to host small conventions here and work with hotels in Fool's Gold to accommodate the overflow of guests. We only take up the basement, which we've remodeled to accommodate our offices, armory and computers."

Sawyer's lips quirked upward on the corners. "And I thought you were just a bunch of mercenaries who worked with what you could only carry on your backs."

"There is always that. But you'll be impressed with how Hank's outfitted this division. I've been up to his digs in Montana, which is on the ranch where he and his wife live. It's impressive."

"I still can't believe Hank married *the* Sadie McClain." Sawyer shook his head. "How does a guy get that lucky? She's a mega star."

"He knew her growing up." Jake grinned. "And you'd be surprised at how down-to-earth she is. She bakes the most incredible cookies and gets down on the floor to play with her children."

"I thought all mega stars had fulltime nannies to raise their children," Sawyer said. "And chefs to provide them with gourmet meals."

"Not Sadie and Hank. Although they do hire a nanny when Sadie has to be on set in LA and Hank can't be with her. But that's not often. Hank does his best to make sure his kids are taken care of by family. And that includes former Navy SEAL, Chuck Johnson, one of the members of his Montana team."

Sawyer's eyes widened. "Chuck Johnson works for Hank?"

"He does." Jake's eyes narrowed. "You know him?"

"He was a legend on my old SEAL team. His heroism is still passed down to new members of the team." Sawyer chuckled. "Wow. I'm impressed. I thought he'd gone to work for the FBI or witness protection, or something like that."

"He had. But then Hank found him and brought him into the brotherhood." Jake tipped his head toward the dining room. "Come on. I'll show you the offices. The door to the basement is in the kitchen."

He led the way through the dining room filled with small and large tables and a buffet against the wall. "Gunny makes a great breakfast for the guests of the lodge. Just so you know, when we're not on assignment, we help out around the ranch. Either way, you're still getting paid, and Gunny gets freed up to tackle some of the chores. It's hard to believe it was just him and RJ running the entire operation *and* the bar next door. We'll have to catch a beer in there sometime soon."

"Sounds good."

Jake pushed through a swinging door into a massive kitchen with racks of pots and pans and a commercial dishwasher. "This is where Gunny makes his magic. You'll like the old Marine. He sounds gruff, but the man is all heart. And he tends to collect stray people."

"Stray people?" Sawyer asked.

"Like Hank, he likes to help out. Since he has a daughter, he's helped out other young women who've needed a hand. You'll get to meet them and some of the other members of our Colorado team soon."

"How many do you have on the team?"

"Counting you? Four." He grinned. "But Hank assures me we're about to hire another five members as soon as he has a chance to get down here and invite them on board."

"Five?"

Sawyer nodded. "Yeah, it's a team of Green Berets who got the shaft. We'll bring everyone up to speed when it's a done deal." He pressed his finger to a print scanner on a pad beside a metal door and waited for the locking mechanism to click. Then he flung open the door and waved a hand. "Welcome to our headquarters."

Sawyer descended the steps into the basement. It had been painted a light color to reflect the bright lights that had been installed throughout, brightening the area. Load-bearing beams had been encased in cedar, giving it a more rustic feel. A long wooden conference table stretched the length of one side of the basement with a huge dry erase board on one side and a giant computer monitor mounted on the wall at the end.

A couple of doors lined another wall. Jake led Sawyer to the first. Again, he scanned his thumb print before he could open the door. As he stepped inside, a light came on automatically.

Shelves and cabinets lined the walls.

"Hank makes sure we have the tools we need to do our job. In here, you'll find communications equipment we might need if we conduct a team operation. We also have GPS trackers we use if we want to keep tabs on our clients." He opened a drawer and took out what appeared to be a necklace. "Maybe not high fashion, but the pendent contains a tracking chip." He handed it to Sawyer and brought out a hand-held device. "You might want Kinsley to wear that necklace. And hold onto this tracker. These mountains can swallow people so fast it's almost scary. I recommend tracking chips to hikers all the time. It's easy to get turned around up here. Before you know it, you're lost, hungry and it gets damned cold."

Sawyer nodded. "I'll get her to wear it."

"Wouldn't be a bad idea for you to carry one, as well." Jake handed Sawyer a small metal disk. "Slip it into your pocket. If you're searching for Kinsley's brother up in the mountains, you might need backup. We might need to find you."

Sawyer slipped the disk and necklace into his pocket then took the tracker and clipped it to his belt.

Jake waved his hand, his gesture encompassing the room filled with equipment and supplies. "We have satellite phones, two-way radios, night-vision goggles and more. If you need any of this, we'll make sure you have it and that it works."

"Good to know," Sawyer said. "I might want to carry a sat phone and get fitted out with two-way radios for me and Kinsley."

"You've got it."

"And I have a vehicle on order. It should be delivered to a dealership in Colorado Springs sometime over the next few days."

"So you said. We can get you there," Jake said.

"In the meantime, Kinsley and I will be in a rental SUV. I'm not sure how rough the roads are we'll be traveling, and I'd hate to damage the rental."

"Some of the roads back in those mountains are nothing more than goat paths. If you encounter those kinds of roads, you're better off trailering the ATVs we have at our disposal in the barn. If it's close to the ranch, you can take horses, if you ride, that is." Jake frowned at Sawyer's arm. "Can you use your left arm at all?"

"I can move it from the shoulder, but from the elbow down…no."

"Four-wheeling might be challenging, but it can be done if your good arm and grip are strong."

Sawyer lifted his chin. "It is. During physical therapy, they stressed how important it was to build up my strength in my remaining, functional limb. I have."

"They don't call these mountains the Rockies for nothing. It can be challenging to keep an ATV on the trail when you come across beds of boulders."

Sawyer pressed his lips together, "I'll manage."

Jake grinned. "I know you will. Have you ever been in the Colorado Rockies?"

Sawyer shook his head. "No. I was born and raised in Texas."

"Ah, a flatlander."

"But I spent time in the hills of Afghanistan, and my team did some mountain and cold-weather training in Alaska."

Jake nodded. "Then you know what to expect and how to prepare for it. Good." He stepped out of the equipment room and waited for Sawyer to follow. Then he closed the door. The lock automatically engaged.

He stepped over to the next room, unlocked it and let Sawyer go first.

The light came on as soon as Sawyer entered. "Wow," he said softly.

Jake chuckled. "Welcome to the armory."

Racks of weapons lined the walls. Rifles, shotguns and handguns of all shapes and sizes.

Sawyer lifted an AR-15 and held it in his hand, testing the weight and feel of the cool metal barrel against his fingertips.

"You know you can still operate one of those," Jake said. "All it takes is a little practice."

If Jake hadn't been standing there, Sawyer would've lifted the rifle to his shoulder, just to feel the strength and beauty of the weapon.

"Gunny set up a firing range up against the mountain. Any time you want to do some target practice, let him know. He'll make sure there aren't any guests wandering around in range."

"Will do." He'd thought his rifle days were over. Maybe...just maybe, they weren't.

"I can assign a handgun to you in the morning. You won't want to be out in the mountains unarmed. You never know what four-legged creature might come after you or your client. And for that matter, you never know what two-legged crazy might do something stupid."

"That's what I'm most afraid of where Kinsley is concerned."

"We'll get the story in the morning. I'd like to video conference Hank when she shares what she knows. Hank's computer guy, Swede, will likely sit in as well. The sooner he can get engaged, the better. He has a way of researching data you didn't know you needed. He's fast and effective."

"Sounds like a plan."

Jake headed for the door. "For now, can I get you set up with a cup of coffee or cocoa?"

"I'd like to get a shower and find my room."

"You got it. RJ will likely be waiting out in the great room to show you to your room. She and Gunny have the running of the lodge down to a science. I don't think there's anything either one of them can't do. From cooking enough food for two hundred people to breaking horses, they're amazing."

Sawyer left the armory and climbed the steps to the kitchen.

"There you are," RJ said with a smile. "I was just making up some hot cocoa. How do you like what they did to the basement?"

"I like it a lot."

She stirred a spoon in a pot on the stove. "And to think it was just a mess of old boxes and junk down there before Hank decided to make it their branch headquarters." RJ pushed a loose strand of her sandy-blond hair back behind her ear. "I don't know what we would've done if they hadn't shown up when they did. Gunny and I were under attack from a local landowner wanting to acquire our place no matter who he had to kill."

"Seriously?" Sawyer shook his head. "What ever happened to good neighbors?"

"The potential to make millions in gold, is what." Her mouth settled into a grim line. "I might still be trapped in an old mine if not for Jake." She took the spoon out of the pot and pointed it at Sawyer. "Stay away from old mine shafts. You never know if the walls are going to cave in or if a lunatic is going to set off an explosion to trap you inside."

Sawyer grinned. "I'll keep that in mind."

"Good." She placed the spoon back in the pot and stirred once more before turning off the heat beneath the pot. "Can I interest you in a cup of homemade hot chocolate?"

"Maybe in a few minutes. I'd like to drop my stuff in my room and grab a shower."

"Of course." She placed a lid on the pot. "It'll still be warm when you come back down. If not, just pour some in a mug and pop it into the microwave." RJ wiped her hands on a towel and turned toward the swinging door. "Follow me."

"I'd like to get my bag and Kinsley's from the SUV, first," he said.

"We already carried your things up to your rooms," RJ said. "Your backpack was all you had, right?"

Sawyer nodded. "Thank you."

"No problem." The woman led the way up the staircase to the landing above.

At that moment, Kinsley came out of a bathroom, wrapped only in a large terrycloth towel. She ground to a stop when she noticed them. "Sorry, I laid out my clothes on my bed and forgot to take them into the bathroom with me." Her cheeks flushed a pretty pink. "Excuse me," she said, and scurried into a bedroom door across the hall.

Sawyer's gaze followed the leggy beauty through the door. His groin tightened at the sight of her toned calves and thighs peeking out from beneath the edge of the towel.

"The lodge is old. Not all the rooms have bathrooms in them. You'll be sharing this one with Kinsley."

Sawyer swallowed hard and nodded. "No problem." Unless he had the same reaction every time he saw her semi-nude in the hallway. She had been a stranger several hours ago, but that didn't mean he was immune to a beautiful woman with gorgeous legs that could easily wrap around a man's body.

He was startled by the kick in the gut of lust she'd inspired. He'd begun to think he'd not only lost the use of his arm, but also the use of...

Sawyer glanced down at the rising ridge beneath the denim of his jeans, relieved and a little embarrassed at how quickly he'd gone from nothing to... well...hard and needy.

"This is your room," RJ was saying as she held open a door. "There are extra towels and toiletries should you need them in the bathroom."

Inside, a queen-sized bed made of rough-hew logs

took up the majority of the room. His backpack had been laid on the quilt covering the bed.

"I'll leave you to it. The cocoa will be waiting when you're ready for it." RJ left him standing inside the door.

Sawyer unzipped his backpack, grabbed his shaving kit and clean clothes and crossed to the bathroom. Minutes later, he was clean, refreshed and wearing a clean T-shirt and jeans. He padded barefooted down to the kitchen, poured cocoa into a mug RJ had left on the counter and carried the mug out onto the front porch. The bright lights had been extinguished, leaving only the one shining beside the front door and the twinkle lights marking the path to the bar.

Sawyer breathed in the fresh-washed air and let the stress of the day slide off his shoulders.

"That's a big sigh," a voice whispered from his left.

He turned and squinted into the shadows.

Kinsley sat on a swing at the far end of the porch, using her foot to push herself back and forth.

Sawyer walked over to stand near her. "I didn't mean to push you into anything you might not want to do."

"Are you kidding me?" She stared up at him over her own mug of cocoa. "I'm grateful for the help. I just hope I can find him quickly so that I don't tie you up too long. Jake and Hank might prefer paying clients to those who can't."

Sawyer shook his head. "You heard what Jake said. Hank isn't in this business for the money. He's in it to help people. It's his and Sadie's way of giving back."

Kinsley stared into her mug. "I wish I didn't have to look for my brother. And when I find him, I'm going to give him a helluva chewing out." She laughed. "After I make sure he's safe."

"At least you won't have to do it on your own."

"For that, I'm eternally grateful. I wasn't even sure where to begin, other than the last place his phone was found on my application."

"We'll start there. Hopefully, there will be people at that location who saw him, or who might give us a clue as to where to look for him."

Kinsley shrugged. "I don't know. I've looked at that location on a map, and it appears to be out in the middle of nowhere. No town nearby…nothing. It's as if he fell off the face of the earth at that point."

"Or into an area with no cell service," Sawyer suggested. "How far is it from Fool's Gold?"

"From what I can tell, it's about a forty-minute drive along some back roads."

"We'll use the computers in the basement and bring it up on the big screen, possibly even a satellite image. I'm sure the Brotherhood Protectors have access to more sophisticated technology."

"That would be nice to do before we head out, but I'd like to get going as soon as possible."

"Jake will contact Hank's computer guy to have him start searching for information on survivalists, anarchists or any other kind of militant organizations in the area."

Sawyer stood at the porch rail, staring out at the stars in the Colorado night sky, feeling more at peace than he had in a long time. He should've felt more on edge, knowing he was on the verge of starting a new chapter in his life. However, being with Kinsley grounded him. Since he'd met her on the plane, he'd felt he wasn't so alone.

The jangle of metal chains sounded beside him. He turned.

Kinsley had risen from the swing and came to stand beside him, resting her mug of cocoa on the porch rail. "I think it was fate that brought us together on that plane," she whispered. "I wasn't sure what I would do once I got to Colorado. I was scared and worried I wouldn't accomplish what I'd come to do. All I could think was that I was one lone woman. How was I going to find my brother? Then I sat down next to you."

He glanced down at her face, bathed in moonlight as she stared out at the mountains and stars shining down on them. "I don't know about fate, but you shouldn't have to do this on your own."

"You didn't have to help me." She touched his good arm. "Thank you."

He reached out and cupped her cheek. "What kind of man would I be if I didn't try?"

She covered his hand with hers. "I've only known you for a few hours, but I can tell without a doubt you're not the kind of man who'd walk away from someone in trouble." Kinsley turned her face and pressed her lips to the palm of his hand.

Heat burned a path from where her hand held his all the way down to his groin. In an instant, he was hard and had the overwhelming urge to crush her in his arms and kiss her until they ran out of air.

Then he remembered he couldn't crush her in his arms because he had only one good arm. And what woman wanted a man who wasn't whole?

Would she be turned off by that fact? Would she feel pity or him? For that matter, was she accepting his help because she felt obligated?

Sawyer dropped his hand to his side. "You know, Jake might have someone with more..." he started to say limbs, but settled for, "experience with finding missing persons. Perhaps you'd rather have someone else help you."

Her eyebrows dipped. "You don't want to help me?"

"No, it's not that. But I'm new. I don't know anything about locating missing persons."

"Neither do I," she said. "But I know you more than I know any of the other men in the Brotherhood

Protectors, even if it's only been for a few hours. I'd rather work with you, if you're okay with that."

"More than okay," he said. "I wouldn't have suggested it to Jake, if I didn't want to do it."

She let go of a breath as if relieved. "Good. I'm glad you'll be with me. I don't know much about getting around in the mountains, or what kind of people I'll run into by myself. Having you with me makes me feel better about everything." She smiled up at him.

Warmth spread through his chest.

Maybe there was something to her claim that fate had had a hand in bringing them together. Whatever it was, he was on board for the ride. At least, until they found her brother.

CHAPTER 4

MORNING LIGHT STREAMED through the window onto Kinsley's face, waking her from a deep sleep. She stretched and opened her eyes, staring up at a sparkling crystal chandelier hanging over her bed. Each crystal seemed to catch the light and shoot rainbow prisms onto the wall beyond.

For a moment, Kinsley couldn't remember where she was and blinked several times to make sure she wasn't still dreaming.

The fog of sleep lifted, and the events of the previous day and night rushed in at her.

She was in Colorado to find her brother, and she had help.

A huge sense of relief was tempered by the thought of the task in front of her.

Colorado was a big state, complicated by the range of mountains running through it. Her brother could be anywhere amongst those peaks. The possibilities were endless and at once overwhelming.

Before she talked herself into a panic attack, she drew in a deep breath and let it out slowly. Then she threw back the quilt, swung her legs over the side of the mattress and let her bare feet settle on the cool wood floor.

She dressed quickly in jeans and a short-sleeved sweater. From the weather app on her phone, she'd noted that the temperatures in Fool's Gold would be fairly warm during the day and cool at night. Dressing in layers made the most sense. She'd wear a jacket over short sleeves and discard it when the air warmed later in the day.

Gathering her toiletries, she crossed the hallway to the bathroom where she performed her morning ablutions, brushed her teeth and pulled her hair back into a ponytail at the base of her neck.

She checked her reflection in the mirror and decided against makeup. Her auburn lashes were dark enough she could forgo mascara. Though her skin was pale, it suited her.

She and her brother didn't look much alike. Which might work in her favor. Where her hair was a dark auburn and wavy, his was sandy-blond and straight, like their father's. Their mother had brown wavy hair. Kinsley had gotten her auburn color and green eyes from her maternal grandmother.

Derek had his father's blue eyes. Though she and

her sibling looked very different, they were close. With an eight-year age difference, Kinsley felt more like a mother, having changed and fed him as a baby.

Her own mother had gone back to work two months after he'd been born. She'd eagerly accepted her daughter's help raising Derek.

Kinsley had promised her mother and father she'd check up on him while they were on their first real vacation they'd taken after they'd both retired. If she failed to find him, she'd be forced to contact the cruise company and get word to them that their son was missing.

She hoped it wouldn't come to that. Kinsley had given herself a personal deadline of two weeks to find him. If it took longer, she would not give up.

After she dropped her toiletries in her room, she passed the room RJ had allotted to Sawyer, slowing briefly, her ears perked for signs that he was on the other side of the door. When she didn't hear any sounds, she moved on and descended the stairs to the main floor of the lodge.

Voices sounded from the dining room.

Several older couples were scattered around the room at various tables, enjoying a meal of eggs, bacon, biscuits and bowls of fruit.

A longer table near the kitchen had been set with plates, silverware and glasses. As yet, no one sat around it, nor was there any food.

The swinging door opened and RJ backed

through it, carrying a pitcher of lemonade and a carafe of coffee. "Good morning," she said as she set the two containers on the table. "We're just about ready to serve up our breakfast. I hope you're hungry."

Kinsley's stomach rumbled at the scents pouring out of the kitchen. "I am. What can I help with?"

"You can carry out the platters of food." RJ led the way back through the kitchen door and held it for Kinsley.

Gunny met them with a tray of fluffy yellow scrambled eggs and another filled with a stack of crispy bacon. "If you two can take these, I need to pull the biscuits out of the oven."

"Got it." RJ removed the tray of eggs from her father's grasp. "Better hurry before you burn this batch."

Kinsley seized the bacon platter.

Gunny spun, grabbed a quilted hot pad, opened the door to the oven and pulled out a tray of piping hot, golden-brown biscuits.

Kinsley's mouth watered, and she groaned. "I was hungry before, but now…" Her stomach growled loudly, making RJ laugh.

"Come on. Let's get you fed before you pass out."

As she turned to the swinging door, the sound of another door opening and heavy feet clumping onto the kitchen's tile floor behind her made Kinsley shoot a glance over her shoulder.

Jake entered, followed by Sawyer, a man with sandy-blond hair and blue eyes and a petite woman with brown eyes and long, dark brown hair pulled back behind her head in a low ponytail.

Gunny set the hot tray on top of the stove. "Perfect timing," he said as he plucked hot biscuits off the tray and dropped them into a cloth-lined basket. "Chow's ready."

"Smells good," the tall blond man said. "What can we do to help?"

"There's a bowl of mixed fruit in the fridge that needs to go on the table. And someone can grab serving utensils or the eggs, fruit and bacon. Also need the butter and jelly out of the refrigerator. Ouch!" Gunny dropped the last biscuit into the basket and shook his hand. "By the way, the woman with the plate of bacon is Kinsley Brothers. I see you've already met Sawyer." Gunny turned to Kinsley and waved a hand at the woman with the dark hair and eyes. "Kinsley, this is JoJo Ramirez."

The small woman snorted. "Call me JoJo." She raised a hand in greeting. "Nice to meet you, Kinsley."

Jake jerked a thumb toward the man behind him. "The big guy with JoJo is Max Thornton, former Green Beret. Also, another member of the Brotherhood Protectors team here in Colorado."

Kinsley dipped her head. "Nice to meet you, too."

"His friends call him Thorn." JoJo slid her arm

around the man's waist and smiled up at him. "On account he's a thorn in their sides."

He narrowed his eyes at her and then bent to press a kiss to her forehead. "It's a good thing I like you."

She cocked an eyebrow and looked up at him. "It's a good thing I like *you*. Who else would put up with you?"

"Good point." He directed his glance toward Kinsley. "She's small but fierce, and I love her."

"Oh," JoJo said. "So, we've just now graduated from like to love?"

"Not hardly. I think I fell in love with you the moment we met."

"Took you long enough to tell me."

"What?" He laughed. "A whole week?"

JoJo pouted. "It felt like forever to me."

"Now, we have the rest of our lives to love each other," he murmured and pressed her close to his side.

Kinsley's heart swelled at the light banter and heavy undertones between the two people. Her gaze met Sawyer's and warmth filled her chest. "Good morning."

"Good morning," he murmured and stepped forward. "I can take the biscuits." He retrieved the basket from Gunny and followed Kinsley through the swinging door. "How did you sleep?"

She smiled. "Better, knowing I wasn't out in the

wilds of Colorado on my own." She laid the bacon platter in the middle of the dining table.

He set the basket of biscuits beside it and straightened.

"Did you get in touch with Hank's computer guy?"

Sawyer nodded. "I did. Swede will be researching this area for potential survivalist or anarchist groups."

Her teeth ground together. "I feel like we need to know so much more."

"And we will. Think of it like eating an elephant."

Kinsley laughed. "How is finding my brother like eating an elephant?"

"At first, it appears impossible and overwhelming. You have to tell yourself that it can be done, and then just do it by eating it one bite at a time."

"Makes sense." She grinned. "The one bite at a time part. Not eating an elephant."

Gunny pushed through the swinging door, carrying a pitcher of orange juice. "Did I hear you want to eat elephant?"

"No," Kinsley chuckled. "I don't want to eat elephant."

"Good," Gunny said with a grin. "Do you know how hard it is to get good elephant meat? It's practically impossible."

"As it should be," RJ said. "I think that's everything. Let's eat. We have a lot to do today, and I'm sure Kinsley and Sawyer want to get an early start."

"Right," Gunny took his seat at the head of the table.

RJ sat at the other end with Jake beside her.

Kinsley liked that Jake didn't try to take the other end of the table since the lodge belonged to Gunny and RJ. He was respectful and made it clear RJ and Gunny were as much in charge of the lodge as he was in charge of his team.

As platters and pitchers made their way around the table, Jake started the conversation. "Where are you starting your search?"

Kinsley glanced toward Sawyer. "I have a point on the map where my phone location application last found my brother's phone. He was working at Breckenridge ski resort until the ski season was over. He let me know he took a job working construction with someone up in the mountains for the summer. That's when the phone calls became more and more infrequent."

Gunny nodded. "It can be hard to get cell reception up in the mountains, depending on where you are."

She pulled up the application that displayed the blue dot of the last location her brother's phone had been detected. She passed the phone to Jake who stared at the dot and enlarged the area to get a better idea of where it might be. "This could be anywhere in a twenty-mile radius."

Kinsley sighed. "I know. But it gives me a starting point. We can also go to Breckenridge and look up the ski resort where he worked in the winter months. Maybe someone will remember my brother and maybe remember who he took a job with."

Jake's eyebrows formed a V over his nose. "That's a lot of maybes."

"I know," Kinsley said, her gazed dropping to the platter of scrambled eggs she held in her hands. She scooped out a small portion onto her plate. "It's not much, but it's all I have. I should've done a better job of asking him for information concerning his place of employment and who he was hanging out with." But then, she'd had a life of her own and a demanding job. A job she'd given up in order to move to Colorado.

After she found her brother, she could apply for work in Colorado Springs or Fool's Gold. Thankfully, she'd saved money for the past few years. Granted, she'd planned on traveling with that money to faraway destinations. But what fun was traveling without a partner to share the experience? So far, she hadn't found any man she would consider as her travel buddy, or anything else for that matter. She'd considered inviting one of her girlfriends along with her, but they'd all married, settled down and had babies. They wouldn't be going anywhere anytime soon. And they wouldn't be going without their husbands or children.

Her travel plans on temporary hold, it didn't bother her to spend the money paying rent while she was jobless, searching for her brother.

What she'd seen of the mountains on both sides of the pass had merit. She'd like living here, if all went well, and she got her brother out of the situation he'd apparently landed in.

And she would. With a little help from a new friend.

She shot a glance in Sawyer's direction. The man chased his eggs around the plate, his lips pressed into a thin line, apparently frustrated that he didn't have another hand available to use his knife to block the eggs from sliding around.

Kinsley plucked a biscuit from the basket in front of her and laid it on his plate in front of the eggs. "Gunny's biscuits are amazing." Then she turned back to her own plate and slathered butter on her own biscuit and took a big bite.

Out of the corner of her eye, she could see Sawyer push the eggs up against Gunny's fluffy biscuit, finally able to capture them and take them to his mouth.

His eyes narrowed, and his lips pressed into an even thinner line.

Kinsley almost regretted placing the biscuit on his plate. The man had pride. He didn't need someone to feed him. Having lost the use of one hand, he had to figure out how to compensate. Others couldn't do it for him. She'd have to remember that. Her natural instinct was to help. Based on the grumpy look on his face, he didn't want her help.

"I know you rented an SUV," Jake was saying, "and it would be fine for starting your search in the mountains, but it might be better if you use one of the company trucks. That way it can't be traced back to you. If your brother is caught up with anyone sophisticated enough, they might be able to trace your rental back to you. Since your last names match, they'll figure out your connection."

"Good point," Kinsley said. "I hate to be any more trouble than I already am, but I'll gladly accept any suggestions or help you want to give. And I can pay you some...but not what you're worth. You see, I saved some money for travel. I'm not working now, so I was hoping to live on that money until I found my brother, then found a job."

Jake was already shaking his head. "No worries. I've already worked it out with Hank. He and Sadie want to take care of this for you."

"I'd like to thank them someday," Kinsley said softly. "They must be very special people to help so many strangers."

Jake nodded. "They are."

When they'd finished eating, everyone helped

carry dishes and platters into the kitchen until the table was empty.

"We'll take care of the dishes," Gunny said. "You two need to get on the road." He shooed Sawyer and Kinsley out of the kitchen.

Jake followed, snagging a set of keys off a hook on the wall. "Take the white crew cab truck parked down by the barn. It's four-wheel drive and will get you most places. If you need to go up old mining trails, you might want to load up some ATVs. Those old roads are barely passable and washed away in many places."

"We're going out to assess the situation and try to come up with leads. If we need ATVs we'll come back and get them," Sawyer said.

Jake nodded. "Good. That will give me time to check them all out and select the best, as well as trailer them for quick deployment."

"Thanks," Sawyer turned to Kinsley. "When can you be ready to leave?"

"Five minutes, tops."

"Same," he said. "I'll meet you out at the barn."

Kinsley ran up the stairs, grabbed her toothbrush and toothpaste and hurried across the hallway to the bathroom. As she brushed, she thought about the day ahead, praying they found her brother and that would be the end of it.

Somehow, she didn't think it would be that easy.

At least she had Sawyer to lean on and assist in her search.

SAWYER HADN'T WANTED to use the ATVs. If they were regular four-wheelers, they'd be difficult to steer one-handed. Already, Kinsley thought he couldn't handle feeding himself. She'd soon be begging for anyone else to assist her. He stood in the dining room, debating his next move when a voice sounded behind him.

"Sawyer, before you go, you might want to see what Hank's guy, Swede came up with." Max stood in the open swinging door to the kitchen.

Sawyer followed the man through the kitchen and down to the basement where one of the computer monitors had the face of a man with white-blond hair and blue eyes staring back at them. He gave them a chin lift when they came into view.

"You must be Sawyer," he said. "I'm Axel Svenson. Most people call me Swede." He shrugged with a grin. "It beats me why."

"Nice to meet you, Swede," Sawyer said.

"I don't know how we missed each other in the Navy. It's not like there are that many of us SEALs out there," Swede said. "You're going to like working with Hank and Jake. Hell, any of the members of our team. We're here to help. You just gotta let us know when you need it."

"I need it. What have you found?" Sawyer got right to the point.

"I searched the web and the dark web for militant organizations in Colorado and got a few hits. There's a group based outside of Durango called *Los Diablos*. I don't think their reach extends this far north or east. They're gang-like and get into trouble selling drugs, stealing cars, robbing liquor stores and now the cannabis distributors. Small-time thugs who dabble in big-time drug dealing. Again, I don't think they're this far north, but they could have come up to Breckenridge to recruit. Mascot tattoos include the image of a devil with curved horns."

Sawyer made a note in his head to be on the lookout for devil tattoos. "What else?"

"In the area northeast of Cripple Creek, is a self-proclaimed survivalist group, that appears to be more anarchist than purely survival oriented. So far."

"Why do you say appear to be anarchist?" Sawyer asked.

"They've been purchasing ammunition and weapons."

"It's not against the law to purchase ammunition and weapons," Sawyer pointed out.

"True, but their members are particularly interested in AR-15s and semiautomatic weapons, not guns used for hunting animals."

"Do you have a location for their compound?" Sawyer asked.

"No. They'd been known to move around to avoid detection. The Department of Homeland Security and the DEA have been following them and lost them on several occasions. They move at night and like to hole up in caves, abandoned mines or abandoned mining towns."

Sawyer frowned. "Any idea how many people are in this organization?"

"DHS guestimates about fifty or sixty."

"That's a lot of people to move," Max noted. "Surely someone is aware of their location."

"Agreed. DHS thinks that many of them are local ranchers disenchanted with the local and national governments. They could be part of the organization, but not living on the compound. They are living in their own homes, providing safe haven for the group's comings and goings."

"Which could make it even harder to get straight answers from people in the area we'll be searching." Sawyer gripped his limp arm. "How militant is this group?"

"For the most part, they're keeping a low profile, from what my contact with DHS reports. I'm still waiting to learn the name of their new leader. I'll let you know as soon as I know. Apparently, they're previous leader died in an ATV accident. Seems his four-wheeler slipped off the edge of a cliff."

"Or was he pushed off the cliff...?" Sawyer didn't

like the sound of the explanation of the leader's death.

"The sheriff and state police investigators didn't find any signs of a struggle. The M.E. reported all the bruising could've happened on his way down."

Sawyer frowned. "Kinsley's brother texted that he wasn't sure how he could get out of the group now that he was in. Is this kind of *accident* the only way out for him?"

Swede shook his head. "The only way to find out is to find someone inside the group willing to talk, spy on the group or infiltrate as potential members."

"Does this group have a name?" Max asked.

Swede stared into Sawyer's eyes. "The Collective."

"Sounds like something out of a science-fiction movie," Sawyer said.

"Yeah, but how often do science fiction movies come to life?" Swede's lip quirked upward on one side. "Think about it. The communicators they flipped open in some of the old sci-fi television shows."

"Flip phones," Max said

"What about the ability to talk to someone and see them at the same time though they're miles, if not light years apart."

"Video conferencing or video phone calls." Sawyer nodded.

"Not that this is a sci-fi movie. What the DHS reports is that The Collective is actively recruiting young people to their cause. They appear to be preppers or survivalists teaching people how to live off the land—until they bring the person into the fold."

Max finished, "And they're brainwashing their new army of followers to their way of thinking and cutting them off from others who might dissuade them from remaining a part of the group. It's a technique used all over the world to build armies out of young, impressionable youths who just want to find a family to belong to. It's how gangs grow in size."

"Wait," Swede clicked his keyboard and frowned as his eyes moved back and forth as if he was reading something. "Just got more information from the DEA. The Collective's leader is a nasty piece of work, who goes by the call sign Blade. He's known to threaten people and follow through on those threats. One young man who managed to escape was found in a friend's apartment in Colorado Springs, completely wrapped like a mummy in duct tape. To include his mouth and nose. He suffocated to death."

"DHS has been working with the DEA to get enough evidence on The Collective to shut them down, but no one will speak out against them," Swede said. "If Kinsley's brother Derek is involved in the Collective, it will be a challenge to extract him. You might need the entire team to get him out alive. And, if he's thoroughly brainwashed, he might resist."

Sawyer's hand gripped his damaged arm as his gaze met Max's.

"You heard Jake," Max said. "We're here for you. All you have to do is let us know you need backup."

"For that matter," Swede added, "the team up here in Montana can be mobilized within a few hours. Just let us know what we can do to help."

Sawyer wasn't sure what he was getting into, or whether he was the right man for the job. All he knew was he couldn't let Kinsley go down the path alone. He should ask Jake to send someone more capable with her. But, by now, he felt he had a stake in her safety. He couldn't let her continue her search without him.

Sawyer gave Swede and Max each a nod. "I'm counting on you should I need assistance."

"You can," Max assured him. "We're a team here at the Brotherhood Protectors. We have each other's six."

"That, we do," Swede seconded.

"Good." Sawyer squared his shoulders. "I'd better get out to the barn. Kinsley will be waiting."

As eager as he was to reunite with the woman he'd met on the plane, he wasn't eager to walk into the lion's den of The Collective with her by his side. It sounded a lot more dangerous than he'd anticipated. And he wasn't so sure he could provide the kind of protection Kinsley might need.

He couldn't go into the situation with a lackluster attitude of *maybe he'd try* to protect her.

His commitment had to be firm.

Sawyer would protect Kinsley with his own life, if it came down to that kind of sacrifice. Even being a lesser man physically than before he'd lost the use of his left arm, he was still the same man inside. He was who he was. If he committed to something as important as saving a life, he'd damn well stand by his word.

CHAPTER 5

Kinsley paced beside a white pickup parked near the large barn behind the lodge. Eager to get on the road to the location on her finder app, she barely noticed the beauty of the Colorado mountains surrounding her.

Then Sawyer rounded the corner of the lodge, striding toward her. Other than his limp arm, he was the image of a strong, healthy former-soldier with broad shoulders and a chiseled chin. His brow dipped as his gaze landed on her.

"Why the frown?" she asked.

"Just spoke with Max and Hank's computer guy, Swede."

"And? Any news?" When he didn't respond immediately, her stomach clenched. "Any good news?" she asked, her voice a little wobbly.

"The area we're heading into has a para-military

anarchists' group called The Collective. They're known for recruiting young people and brainwashing them into joining their cause."

"And what is their cause?" She had to ask the question, but didn't really want to know the answer.

"Most anarchist groups resist government authority. If they had their way, they'd establish their own governments and secede from the US."

Kinsley pressed a hand to her breast. "I can't imagine Derek agreeing to be in an organization like that. For the most part, he's been a rule-follower."

"That's just it. They take people who might have issues fitting in, or who are lonely, and target them. They make them feel like they belong, while indoctrinating them into their ways of thinking." He walked around to the passenger door of the truck.

Kinsley followed. "You said *paramilitary*. Are they dangerous?"

"They can be. Like preppers, they stockpile enough food, supplies, guns and ammunition to survive in the case of a breakdown in government or infrastructure." Sawyer opened the door for her.

As she climbed up on the running board, she turned to Sawyer, her eyes level with his. He was standing so close she could feel the heat of his body. Her own senses responded, sending fire through her veins to pool low in her belly. She touched a hand to her chest, in an ineffective attempt to slow her heartbeat. "Did Swede know where we could look for these people?"

Sawyer met her gaze. "Northeast of Cripple Creek."

She brought up the image she'd saved of the last location of her brother's cellphone and stared at the names of the towns surrounding the blue dot. Her pulse quickened. "That's the last place my app found Derek's cellphone." She scooted onto the passenger seat. "Let's go."

Sawyer's frown deepened. "It could get danger-ous," he warned.

"I expected that." Kinsley lifted her chin. "What kind of sister would I be if I didn't go after my brother, danger or not?"

"A live sister. Why don't you notify the local law enforcement in that area?"

"I checked with the Colorado State Police. They sent someone to his last known residence in Breck-enridge. He'd checked out of his furnished apartment and turned in his keys. The apartment manager spoke to him, and he seemed okay. No foul play suspected. Since he didn't leave a forwarding address, they didn't know where to go from there. They got busy with other cases and dropped mine. That's when I decided to come out here and search for myself."

Sawyer closed her door and rounded the truck to slide into the driver's seat. He started the engine, pulled away from the barn and drove down the gravel road to the highway leading into Fool's Gold.

At the stoplight, he turned left and headed southwest, passing the shops and restaurants making up the tiny tourist town.

Kinsley made note of the sheriff's station. She might stop there and leave an image of her bother with them in case they came across Derek in the backwoods. They passed a Bed and Breakfast, Mattie's Diner, a florist shop named Laurel's Florals, a small hospital or medical clinic, an Ice cream shop and all the usual places found in a small tourist town. At the western end of Fool's Gold, was the original, or a reconstruction of the original mining town, made out to be a kind of old west, or ghost town. It was quaint with false storefronts and a saloon with swinging doors.

If Kinsley wasn't so worried about Derek, she'd find Fool's Gold to be a friendly town and one she'd like to visit in better circumstances.

Soon enough, they'd left the little town and drove out into the countryside where grassy fields were backed by tree-covered hills and the backdrop of a huge mountain, towering above everything.

The majesty of the mountain and the neighboring peaks made Kinsley catch her breath. Her first time this far west, it was also the first time she'd been to the Rocky Mountains. Her heart swelled at the beauty of her surroundings.

"Is that Pike's Peak?" she asked, pointing to the south.

He nodded. "It's over 14,100 feet high."

"Is it the highest peak? I should know my geography better."

Sawyer shook his head. "Not even in the top ten. I think it's number twenty."

"Wow. There are that many tall mountains in this state?"

"Yup. Mount Elbert is the tallest in Colorado at 14,440. Don't ask me the other eighteen in between."

"How do you know even that much?"

He shot her a wry smile. "We conducted a mountain training exercise in conjunction with the 10th Special Forces out of Ft. Carson. One of the trivia questions involved knowing the tallest mountain in the state."

"Must be nice to live and work out here."

"I always wanted to return. Though I love the beaches and water around Coronado, California, my trip to the Rockies never left me. I could never get tired of the views and the clean, crisp mountain air," Sawyer commented.

"I can see why. Seeing all of this…" she waved a hand at the mountains and valleys, "makes me understand how people love it so much out here. And you're right, it's nothing like the coastlines of Georgia, Texas or California."

"If you stay in Colorado, where will you land?" Sawyer asked.

Kinsley shrugged. "I liked the look of Fool's Gold. I could see myself working at the hospital there, or maybe a clinic. If there isn't a job there, I could find work in Colorado Springs. It's large enough and has a significant number of medical facilities."

"You could live in Fool's Gold and commute to the Springs. It's only a thirty-minute drive."

"Which wouldn't be bad. I spent at least thirty minutes in traffic getting to and from work in Savannah, and it was only seven miles and twenty traffic lights."

"It would mean going through the pass twice a day," he said. "It's not bad when the weather isn't making the road conditions treacherous."

"And how often is that?"

"Not terribly often. They get snow in the winter, but not as much as in the northeastern states."

"I could live with it. Not that we get snow in Savannah, but I've visited New Hampshire and Vermont in the winter to ski. I'm looking forward to skiing in the Rockies. I see why my brother fell in love with it."

"You left your job to move out here. Wasn't that a little bit of overkill? I mean, surely, they would've given you a leave of absence or paid time off."

She shot a glance out of the side window. "I was ready to leave Savannah."

A long silence stretched between them.

"Bad relationship?" He glanced her way. "You don't have to answer, if you don't want to. It's none of my business."

She sighed. "It's okay. It's over. Heck, it was over a long time ago. I just didn't see the signs. Apparently, I was too busy establishing myself in my field to give our relationship and my ex-boyfriend the attention they deserved."

"And he found someone else?" Sawyer asked quietly.

Kinsley nodded. The ache of betrayal still pinched her chest. But she'd discovered it was really a hit to her ability to trust. "What's sad is that I'm not heartbroken." She glanced across the console toward a man who'd been a stranger less than twenty-four hours ago. "I don't know why I'm telling you this. You could probably care less."

"It's filling the drive time," he said. "Tell me this... If your ex would take you back as if he'd never met another woman, would you go back to him?"

"No," she said without hesitation. "I think I was more in love with the idea of having a steady boyfriend and the potential of starting a family than I was in love with Jason."

"Did you have much in common with him?" he asked, his lips quirking upward on the corners.

She smiled, recalling the conversation they'd had driving down from Denver. "More than you and I do, it seems. He's a doctor. I'm a PA. We work in the medical field and speak the same language...medical. We could discuss cases, diagnosis and treatments all day long."

"But there wasn't any spark?" He shot a glance her way, meeting her gaze for a split second before he returned his attention to the road.

Again, she sighed. "No. I'm not sure there ever was. We were both practical and dedicated to our work."

"And the new girlfriend spends more time with him outside of work, not talking about medicine and treatments?"

Kinsley's mouth twisted. "She's a bartender."

"And a good listener."

"Yeah." Kinsley stared out the front window. "And I'm not."

"You've been a good listener with me," he pointed out.

"Because we haven't once spoken about medical cases, treatments or anything to do with work."

"That could be it."

"I know." She glanced down at her hands, clasped in her lap. "I make a terrible girlfriend."

"I wouldn't say that," Sawyer said. "You didn't have the right boyfriend."

"True. But the thought of starting over makes me stressed. I don't like the idea of dating someone I've only met online, and I'm not into going to the gym to meet men. They're sweaty and too interested in muscle-building than having real conversations."

He laughed. "You might have a point. What about joining a hiking club? I'm sure there are lots of interesting people here in Colorado who like to hike."

She nodded. "It's a possibility. But first, I have to find Derek."

"And we will," Sawyer said, his tone firm, his jaw tight.

"I hope so," she said. "I hope he's all right. I helped raise that kid. He's more than a little brother to me."

"I felt that way about my sister, until she met and married her husband. Now, she's happily working, raising children and busy being a soccer mom. She doesn't need me anymore. She has an entire life I'm not a part of."

"That's what I'm afraid of with Derek. I just hope that his life doesn't include being a part of a fanatical anarchists' group."

The rest of the drive to Cripple Creek was spent in silence. The closer they got to the little mining town, the more antsy Kinsley grew.

"We should stop at the sheriff's office first," she said. "I want to show them a picture of Derek. Maybe they've seen him around town. If not, I want to leave an image of my brother with them so they can be on the lookout for him."

"Can do," Sawyer said.

Minutes later, they pulled into the little town. The

stores and businesses appeared just like they had in the late 1800s, maybe with more paint and paved roads in front of them. Other than that, Kinsley felt like she'd stepped into the past.

The sheriff's department was in one of the old buildings. Sawyer pulled into the parking lot beside it and got out of the truck.

Kinsley slid down from her seat and met him at the rear of the vehicle. She pulled a sheet of paper out of her purse and unfolded it. On the paper was a picture of a young man with blond hair and blue eyes.

Sawyer took the paper and studied the image. "He really doesn't look much like you, does he?"

Her lips twisted. "No, he doesn't. When he was little, everyone mistook me as the babysitter, not his sister. But we're siblings, and I love him."

Sawyer glanced toward the sheriff's office. "This is a small town, and you don't know where people align, even the law enforcement. Why don't you let me handle this?"

"Do you think the sheriff might be working with the anarchists' group?"

"I don't think anything. But it might be better if we approach this as other than a sister looking for her brother."

She frowned up at him. "What do you suggest?"

"Do you trust me?"

She laughed. "If I don't trust you by now, I'd be an

idiot. We drove down from Denver together. You could easily have shoved a knife in my throat and dumped my body on the side of the road."

Sawyer's eyes widened. "That was graphic."

"Sorry," she said. "But it's true. I trust you. You seem to be a guy on the up and up."

"Glad you feel that way."

She leaned close and lowered her voice, a sparkle in her eye. "So, what's our cover, Sherlock."

He liked that she had a mischievous gleam in her deep green eyes. "Follow my lead."

Holding the door open to the building, he waited for her to pass through then entered behind her.

A woman met them at the front desk. "May I help you?" she asked.

Sawyer glanced at the nameplate on the woman's desk. "Ms. Bippert, we're looking for this young man." He handed the sheet of paper to the woman behind the desk. "We were hoping the sheriff or one of the deputies might have seen him."

Ms. Bippert took the sheet of paper from his hands and stared down at Derek's smiling face. "Nope. I haven't seen him. I can pass this photo around the department and inquire if anyone else might have spotted him." She laid the paper on the desk and looked up at Sawyer and Kinsley, her pen poised over a notepad. "Who is he, and why are you looking for him?"

"He's my—" Kinsley started.

Sawyer cut in. "He's our former renter. He skipped out of his apartment without paying the last month's rent. We're not looking for trouble, just for the money he owes us."

"Lot of that going on in the resort towns," the woman grumbled. "They spend like there's no tomorrow during ski season, and when the summer rolls around, they're out of work and still spending like they're working." She snorted. "I'll be sure to circulate the picture. What's his name?"

Sawyer turned to Kinsley.

"Derek Brothers," Kinsley said. "We just want our money. No drama or trouble."

"I'll let the sheriff know to be on the lookout for him." Ms. Bippert looked past them. "Speak of the devil…"

Kinsley and Sawyer turned to find a man with brown eyes and a ruggedly handsome face, wearing a sheriff's uniform and a cowboy hat, entering the building. He appeared to be younger than Kinsley would have expected, but then she wasn't familiar with small-town life or elected officials.

He took off his hat and ran a hand through his dark brown hair. "Did I hear my name?"

"Sheriff Jones," Ms. Bippert handed the paper to him, "these people are looking for a Derek Brothers. They say he owes them money for rent after he skipped town without paying."

The sheriff glanced down at the picture, his brow

furrowing. "And why do you think he might be in this area?"

"He mentioned to one of the other apartment tenants that he was headed to Cripple Creek to get a job at one of the casinos," Sawyer said, the lie flowing off his tongue like the truth.

Kinsley's gut knotted. She'd never been good at lying, and doing so to an officer of the law would have been impossible. So, she kept her mouth shut and let Sawyer do the talking.

"I haven't seen him," the sheriff said, handing the paper back to Sawyer.

Sawyer passed it to the woman at the desk. "We'd appreciate it if you'd circulate it among your deputies and call us if you see him around." He took a pen out of cup on the desk and wrote a telephone number on the paper beside the picture of Derek. "Day or night. Don't hesitate. He owes us."

"We can't get money out of him, if that's what you want," the sheriff said. "You'll have to take him to small claims court, if you find him."

"That's just it," Sawyer said. "We can't take him to court if we don't know where he is. Any help would be appreciated."

"Are you staying in Cripple Creek?" the sheriff asked.

"No, we secured lodging in Fool's Gold. We can be here in less than forty minutes. If we need to, we can secure lodgings here in Cripple Creek."

"Fool's Gold is close enough. If this kid is running from you, it might be better to base out of a town nearby, not here. That is, if he's in this area," the sheriff said. "We'll notify you if we see him."

"Thanks." Sawyer held out his good hand.

When the sheriff reached out to shake it, Sawyer tipped his chin toward the other man's arm where an eagle, a globe and an anchor were tattooed on his forearm. "Prior service?"

The sheriff's eyes narrowed, and he nodded. "Marine Corps."

Sawyer lifted the sleeve of his T-shirt to expose the Navy SEAL trident on his left bicep. "Navy. Thank you for your service."

"Same to you. Ooh-rah."

Sawyer grinned. "Hoo-yah." He turned and walked through the door, holding it for Kinsley as she exited the sheriff's department.

Once they were inside the pickup with the doors closed, Kinsley frowned at Sawyer. "What was that all about? Why did you lie to the sheriff?"

"I don't know who's a good guy and who might be a bad guy in this town."

"Cripple Creek has a ton of visitors every year. Surely, the sheriff has a handle on what's going on around here."

"Since when have casinos had squeaky clean reputations? Where there's money, there's crime."

"But the sheriff is prior military. Don't you all look out for each other?" She shook her head.

"Not all military men and women are trustworthy. I've known soldiers who would sell their souls to the devil for fifty bucks. And I've known members of my SEAL team who would lay down their lives to save mine or any other member of our team. You never know until you know for sure. The sheriff might be one of the good guys. But we can't be sure. Therefore, I'm not giving him any more information than I already have. And I sure as hell don't want anyone here to link you with Derek Brothers. So, while you're in Cripple Creek, we're Sawyer and Kim Johnson."

"As in Mr. and Mrs.?" Her heart turned a somersault, and then beat madly against her ribs.

"Yes. We'll be seen together, asking about Derek Brothers. If he's around, and word gets back to him that the Johnsons are looking for him, he won't know who that is and blurt out that Kinsley is his sister's name."

Kinsley nodded. "Okay. We don't want to put him in any more danger than he might already be in."

"Or put you in danger because you're looking for your brother. The Collective, if that's the group he's mixed up in, will try to keep him from any family members. They might also hide him from bill collectors, but better that than putting a target on you.

They might decide to use you as incentive to keep Derek in line."

"I never thought of that." She ran a hand through her hair. "This is so out of my league. I don't know what to do."

"We'll find your brother. Once we do, we'll figure out how to bring him home."

She squared her shoulders. "Where to from here?"

"To the location on your app and then to a local diner around here," Sawyer said. "We need to go where the locals hang out. The people of The Collective have to eat, too. If they're in town, they'll go to the diner. If they need supplies, they'll hit the hardware and grocery stores. We can do our own search without the help of the sheriff's department. And if the sheriff is in cahoots with The Collective, he'll get word to them that someone is looking for the kid."

"Won't that make them hide him deeper in the backwoods or mountains?"

Sawyer pulled out of the parking lot at the sheriff's department and drove slowly down Main Street. "Possibly. But it will also make them watch us. If we can find the folks watching us, we can watch them and follow them back to wherever they've set up camp."

"Seems to me we need to secure lodging here in Cripple Creek, if this is the nearest town to where The Collective is operating," Kinsley said.

"We don't know that yet. If we get any inkling

that this is the place The Collective uses to resupply, we will get a room here. For all we know, they might be operating out of Cañon City, Breckenridge or even Fool's Gold."

"But this was the last place my brother's phone showed on my finder app," Kinsley said. "He has to be somewhere nearby. We haven't even gone to the location where it last found him."

"We're going now." Sawyer pulled out his cellphone and brought up a map of the area. "Swede did his best to match the coordinates to your app. Since it's only a needle in a haystack, we'll drive out that way and see what we find."

Kinsley's breath hitched, and her heart hammered. Since leaving her home in Savannah, she'd been hellbent on getting to the blue dot indicated on the map. It was all she had to go on in her quest to locate her brother. A million scenarios rushed through her head.

Would they find Derek? Would he be there? Would they find his cellphone and not him? Would they find his body decomposing in a ditch…?

She closed her eyes and sent a silent prayer to the heavens. *Let Derek be there, and please, Lord, let him be alive.*

CHAPTER 6

Sawyer drove the truck out of Cripple Creek, heading northeast on a county road. For the first couple of miles, they passed concrete driveways into properties with fences and electric gates barring entrance. Some of the driveways weren't blocked, but led up steep, gravel roads to homes perched on rocky knolls, peeking through the trees.

The further they traveled along the county road, the driveways became less frequent, until the road turned from pavement to gravel, and they still weren't to the location where the cellphone was last located.

"I'm surprised his phone had any reception this far out of town." Kinsley glanced down at her screen. "I have only one bar of reception, and it's blinking in and out as we round curves in the road."

"It could be that he had just enough reception to

transmit his location before he moved out of the cell tower's area."

She looked up. "Slow down. We should be getting close."

He brought the truck to a crawl and rolled to a stop before the road curved around a huge outcropping of rocks. On one side was the mountain, stretching upward, too steep even to climb without special equipment. On the other side of the road, the ground dropped down a steep slope over two-hundred feet to a rocky ravine below.

The road had been blasted out of the rocks, not much more than a rocky ledge, wide enough for one vehicle to round the curve at a time.

Kinsley opened her door and looked out. Her face paled, and she closed the door again. "I hope there's a place to turn around ahead of us, because the road isn't wide enough to do that here. Are you getting out?"

He rested his hand on the doorhandle. "I'd like to look around and see if we can find your brother's cellphone in this vicinity."

"Me, too," she said. "If we get out, we need to do so on your side of the truck. We're close to the edge on this side."

She didn't say it, but Sawyer could see in her face that she wasn't comfortable stepping out onto the gravel where one turn of the ankle could send her plummeting to the bottom of the hill.

Sawyer shifted into park and left the engine running. He stepped out of the vehicle and waited for Kinsley to scoot across the console to the driver's seat and drop down onto the running board.

He held out his hand for her as she dropped to the ground. She leaned into him for a moment, her face pressed to his chest.

He slipped his arm around her back and held her there.

"Did I tell you I'm afraid of heights?" she murmured. Her breath warmed his chest through the fabric of his T-shirt.

His gut clenched and his groin tightened. "No, you didn't."

"Well, I am." She drew in a deep breath, let it out and squared her shoulders. "Okay. Let's see if that cellphone is around here somewhere."

She took a step away from him toward the uphill side of the road and looked closely at the rocks and gravel in the crevice that served as a drainage conduit.

While she searched that side of the road, Sawyer looked over the edge to the bottom of the steep drop. As far as he could tell, there weren't any bodies down there. Whether or not there was a cellphone…well, they'd have to wonder.

Sawyer couldn't climb down without rappelling gear and others to help belay and bring him back up. One-armed men were challenged in the mountains.

Yes, he'd seen climbers who had only one arm. But he wasn't quite there in his rehabilitation to tackle that kind of terrain. Though, if he had to, he'd do it. He'd figure out a way. If lives depended on him. If Kinsley's life depended on it, he'd do anything, including scaling the side of a mountain. He hoped it didn't come to that anytime soon.

"Nothing," he heard her say. "See anything?" she asked, inching up to where he stood at the edge of the road. "Please say no."

He reached for her hand and held it securely in his. "Nothing. I doubt we'd see a cellphone that far down. And no, I don't see your brother."

She let go of a long, shaky breath. "At least there's a chance of finding him alive."

"Let's see what's around the corner," Sawyer said.

She nodded and held tightly to his hand.

"You might want to walk on the uphill side," he said, knowing he couldn't hold her hand on that side.

Kinsley nodded and switched sides, looping her arm around his.

He clamped her hand between his upper arm and the side of his chest since his hand was unable to move or hold onto hers. He hated that he couldn't use it, but she didn't seem to mind and wasn't revolted by his disability.

"Thank you for humoring me," she said softly as they walked along the gravel road and rounded the huge escarpment.

When they finally got all the way around the rocky outcropping, they came to an abrupt halt.

A hundred yards ahead was a metal gate blocking the road ahead. Chain link fence stretched out on both sides, going up the slope of the mountain and down the other side with spirals of concertina wire on top. A sign on the fence gave a grim message.

NO TRESPASSING
VIOLATERS WILL BE SHOT

KINSLEY'S BODY shook against Sawyer's.

"We don't know that your brother is inside that fence." Sawyer reached over to cover Kinsley's hand with his.

A cloud of dust appeared around the corner of another curve in the gravel road ahead. A black pickup seemed to materialize out of it. On the back of the truck was what appeared to be a machinegun mounted on a post with a man holding onto it.

The truck skidded to a halt behind the gate.

Kinsley backed up half a step. "What the hell?"

The passenger climbed out of the cab of the truck, carrying an AR-15 semi-automatic rifle. He wore a black body armor vest loaded with magazines that Sawyer had to assume were filled with bullets. The man lifted his chin and stared down his nose at Kinsley and Sawyer. "Can't you read?"

Sawyer stiffened. "Yes, we can."

The man with the rifle took a step toward the gate. "Then leave."

"We're not trespassing," Sawyer stated, without any inflection, no sarcasm, nothing. He wasn't there to start a fight, and he wouldn't. Not with Kinsley standing beside him.

"We don't like people hanging around our property."

"We're just looking for someone we thought might have come out this way," Sawyer said.

"Who are you looking for?"

"Derek Brothers," Sawyer said. "He owes us money."

Their emissary's jaw tightened, but he gave no other sign that he recognized the name. "Never heard of him."

The guy with his hands on the machinegun shifted from one foot to the other, his eyes narrowing as he swiveled the barrel of the weapon, aiming it at Sawyer's chest.

"Go back to the truck," Sawyer said, his tone low, barely loud enough for her to hear, and definitely not loud enough for the guy with the rifle to hear over the sound of his truck's engine.

"I'm not leaving without you," she whispered.

"Just do it. I'll be right behind you." He glanced

down at her. "I promise."

She stared up at him a moment longer and then gave him an imperceptible nod. Turning her attention to the welcoming committee, she waved. "Thank you for your hospitality." Then she performed an about-face and marched back to the truck.

Sawyer knew how hard it was for her, given her fear of heights, and coupled with the fact there was a loaded machine gun pointed at her back.

Sawyer stepped between the barrel of the machine gun and Kinsley. "We'll just be on our way. Thank you for your time."

As he turned, the man with the rifle spat on the ground. "Don't bother to come back. We won't be so welcoming next time."

Sawyer gave him a mock salute. "I'll keep that in mind." He walked back around the bluff to find Kinsley waiting on the other side, not inside the truck like he'd asked her to. He reached out his hand and took hers in his. They reached the truck without being stopped.

Once inside, Sawyer glanced at the rocky bend in the road to find the man with the rifle standing there, his weapon held out in front of him, his steely stare boring a hole into them.

"How are we going to get down this road?" Kinsley asked. "We can't turn around."

He shifted into reverse. "We'll back down to a point where we can turn around."

"Sweet Jesus, help us," she whispered beneath her breath.

"Close your eyes. What you can't see won't hurt you." Sawyer gripped the steering wheel and looked over his shoulder. He backed down the narrow road an inch at a time, moving slowly so that he didn't inadvertently drive off the edge of a cliff. They'd gone a quarter of a mile before he found a wide spot large enough to allow them to turn around. Once they were heading down the mountain, he let go of the breath he'd been holding, glanced over at Kinsley and chuckled.

"You can open your eyes now."

"No, I can't. Not until we're all the way down this damned mountain."

"Okay. I'll let you know." He drove the rest of the way down the narrow dirt road. When they made it to the paved surface, the ground leveled out, and they came out into an area of open fields and grassland. "We're down."

She opened her eyes and stared out the front windshield. "Were those people part of The Collective?"

Sawyer nodded. "That would be my guess."

He was worried. Very worried.

The men on and in that truck meant business. They wouldn't hesitate to shoot if someone wandered into their territory.

. . .

KINSLEY'S HEART sank to the pit of her belly. "Dear Lord," Kinsley said softly. "What has my brother gotten himself into?"

"If he's on that property, it will be a challenge to extract him."

"How?" She looked up at him, overwhelmed by what that fence and those men with guns meant. "They could be holding him prisoner. How are we supposed to get past them to Derek? You heard them. They'll shoot anyone who steps onto their land."

Sawyer's mouth twisted. "I've been in tougher situations. The difference was I had a team at my six."

Kinsley's brow wrinkled. "At your six?"

"They had my back and I had theirs. Point is, we worked as a team."

"But you were a Navy SEAL. You trained with your team." She wrung her hands in her lap. "Out here...you're just you. We're not trained as a team, and there's just you and me."

Sawyer's jaw tightened. "And the Brotherhood Protectors, all of whom have served in Special Forces, whether as Navy SEALs, Green Berets or MARSOC."

"MARSOC?" Kinsley's head was spinning. She couldn't get past the image of the machinegun being pointed at them from the back of the pickup.

"MARSOC stands for Marine Corps Forces Special Operations Command. They're the Marines' special operations units."

"How are they going to help us here?" Kinsley's heart raced, and her breathing was ragged. If she didn't get a grip on her emotions, she'd hyperventilate and be of no use to her brother. Forcing herself to take a deep, steadying breath, she turned to Sawyer. "What are we going to do?"

"We still haven't determined whether or not your brother is on that compound."

"How are we going to find out?"

"I'd like to question more people in town. If anyone has seen him, they might know where he is."

"As in, with The Collective?" Kinsley asked.

"Exactly. The locals might know who belongs to the group at the end of that road. It might not even be The Collective. It could be an entirely different militant group. If your brother isn't with them, we have no need to infiltrate their compound."

"I'd prefer not to cross that line, if at all possible."

"Same," Sawyer said with a crooked grin. "I don't care to have a loaded machinegun pointed at my chest any more than you do."

"Okay. Let's go back to town and find out all we can. Hopefully, we were headed in the wrong direction on that road up the mountain." She prayed she was right, though her gut told her otherwise.

She sat in strained silence the rest of the way back to Cripple Creek until Sawyer pulled up in front of a diner with a decent crowd of vehicles filling the parking lot.

"This must be where the locals eat." Sawyer shifted into park and killed the engine. He dropped down out of the truck and started around to her side.

Kinsley sat for a moment, reminding herself to breathe.

Sawyer opened her door and smiled gently at her. "You've never had a loaded gun pointed at you, have you?"

She shook her head, her eyes filling. "No, and you have?" Kinsley choked on a laugh. "Of course, you have. You were a Navy SEAL." She stared at him, her brow scrunching. "How did you deal with it?"

"By taking one breath at a time and focusing on my mission."

Kinsley blinked back the tears and nodded. "That's what I need to do. Focus on my brother and getting him out of whatever hellhole he's landed in."

"First…we find him." Sawyer held out his hand. "Come on, Mrs. Johnson. Let's have lunch with the locals and see what we come up with."

When he called her Mrs. Johnson, a warm flush welled up her neck and filled her cheeks. The man made the name sound as natural, as if it were real.

"Now might not be the time to ask," she said as she took his hand, "but is there a Mrs. Johnson?"

She held her breath, waiting for his response.

He grinned. "Yes, of course."

A deep sense of disappointment flooded through her chest. As soon as she was steady on her feet, she released his hand as if it were scalding hot. "I'm sorry. I didn't realize..."

He laughed and rested his arm at the small of her back, urging her toward the door to the diner. "Mrs. Johnson was my mother. But for our purposes today, you're the only Mrs. Johnson." He winked down at her. "I'm not married," he whispered.

Relief washed over her. "Were you ever?"

He shook his head.

Her eyes rounded. "Why not? You're a good-looking man. A number of women must have been vying for your proposal."

Sawyer grimaced. "I didn't have time. When we weren't deployed three hundred days out of the year, we were training for those deployments. I barely had time to date any woman more than once." He opened the door to the diner and held it for her to enter.

A waitress walked by at that moment. "Find a seat. I'll be with you in a minute."

Sawyer guided Kinsley to a booth in a corner. "If you don't mind, I'd like to sit with my back to the wall," he said.

Kinsley nodded and took the seat across from the one against the wall. "Do you think anyone will come in armed?"

"No. But I like to watch people coming and going to get an idea of what the folks are like."

Kinsley frowned. "For that matter, I'd like to sit with my back to the wall, as well."

Sawyer waved toward the bench seat and waited for her to move from where she was to the inside of the booth. Then he settled beside her.

The waitress arrived with two laminated menu cards and two glasses of water. "I'm Amy. I'll be your server. Would you like anything else to drink?"

Kinsley smiled at Amy. "No thank you."

"I'd like coffee," Sawyer said.

Amy left them to peruse the menu while she went for the cup of coffee.

After a quick glance at the menu, Sawyer's gaze swept the diner.

Kinsley decided on a club sandwich, and then studied the patrons of the diner.

An older couple sat in the booth next to theirs. Four men occupied a table in the middle of the diner, discussing the latest national news, from what Kinsley could hear of their conversation.

A young woman sat with a man, holding his hand across the table, smiling into his eyes.

Kinsley couldn't help but smile at them. How nice would it be to sit across the table from Sawyer, holding his hand without a care in the world? She could imagine staring into his eyes with that look of adoration and love.

Since they'd met, he'd been kind, generous and caring of her comfort and safety. It hadn't all been because she was his client. He'd been that way before they'd made it to Lost Valley Ranch. Nothing had changed when he'd insisted on her mission to find her brother being his first assignment. He was still kind, considerate and concerned about her safety. He'd proven that in front of those men with the guns. Instead of antagonizing them, he'd played his hand lowkey and steady until he could get her out of harm's way.

And he'd held her when she'd been scared of the drop-off. He hadn't needed to do that. It was who he was, and he probably acted that way with everyone.

He'd talked about how his team had his back and he had his team's back.

Kinsley's heart swelled. That the man had remained unmarried for so long was a miracle. He was every woman's dream.

She stared at the hand beside her. The one that no longer worked for Sawyer. He probably thought of himself as less of a man because of it.

Kinsley thought of him as more of a man as he fought to establish a new normal life for himself. He'd shown remarkable courage for taking on a job that most men would find too dangerous. From what she'd gathered about the Brotherhood Protectors, they did more than just play bodyguard to rich socialites. They were involved in operations that put them at risk of being killed. They had to use every bit of their training as special forces operatives to survive and keep their clients alive.

Amy arrived with the mug of coffee and set it in

front of Sawyer. Then she pulled a pad and pencil out of her apron and smiled. "What would you like?"

Kinsley ordered the club sandwich. Sawyer ordered the same and handed the menus to Amy.

A man entered the restaurant as Amy turned toward the kitchen. He wore black jeans and a black T-shirt with the sleeves rolled up to the tops of his shoulders. His arms were covered with garish tattoos of buxom women, dragons and swords. On his right forearm was the same tattoo of a globe, eagle and anchor the sheriff had on his forearm.

Kinley leaned toward Sawyer. "Isn't that the same tattoo as the one on Sheriff Parker's arm?"

Sawyer nodded. "It stands for the Marine Corps."

The man's short hair was spiked straight up, and he sported a beard.

"Hey, Marion," Amy called out. "The usual?"

He frowned at the waitress. "Don't call me that."

"Why? It's your name, isn't it?" She smirked. "Oh, wait. You wanted me to call you something else, didn't you? Marion wasn't good enough for you."

The man snarled. "Shut up and get me some coffee."

Amy cocked an eyebrow. "Say please."

He glared at her.

"Give him his coffee," a large man in a white apron called out from the swinging door to the kitchen. "I'll have his order out to him in a second so he can get out of here."

Marion straddled a stool at the counter and tapped his fingernails against the laminate. "You heard Cookie. Get me my coffee."

"Lola," Amy called out to the waitress on the other side of the diner. "I'm going on break. Will you get this jerk a coffee?"

Marion grabbed Amy's arm and yanked her toward him, wrapping his arm around her and trapping her hands to her side. "Don't get sassy with me. You been sniffing round my spawn, again? I told him to lay off."

Sawyer stiffened beside Kinsley.

"Or what?" Amy said. "You think you're so tough because you threaten people?" She stared at him. "You don't scare me, Marion. You're nothing but a bully, and I'm calling you on it."

Marion tightened his hold around her middle until she squirmed. "Let go of me," she said, her voice breathy as if she wasn't getting enough air.

Sawyer was out of his seat and across the floor in a second. He laid his hand on Marion's shoulder. "I believe the lady told you to let go."

Marion stared at the hand on his shoulder and then up at Sawyer.

Kinsley left her seat and moved toward Sawyer and the bully. She wasn't sure how she could help, but she wouldn't stand by and do nothing if the situation got out of hand.

"Get your filthy hand off me," Marion growled through bared teeth.

"My hands are clean," Sawyer said in an even tone. "I'll let go of you when you let go of Ms. Amy."

"I'll do whatever the hell I please," Marion said. "Now, get your hand off my shoulder before I mop the floor with you."

"If you're going to mop the floor with me, then you'll have to release the young lady first."

Marion glared at Sawyer.

Kinsley reached for a glass jar of sugar on a nearby table. It was the only thing heavy and hard enough close by that she could use as a weapon.

Sawyer's muscles bunched, ready for Marion's next move.

The tattooed man shoved Amy away, spun off of his stool, popped open a wicked looking knife and made a swipe at Sawyer.

Kinsley gasped.

Sawyer was ready and dodged the blade easily.

When Marion only stabbed air, he roared in anger and jabbed again.

Sawyer stepped to the side, grabbed the man's wrist and shoved it high. Then he kneed the man in the groin.

When Marion doubled over, Sawyer jerked his wrist down and spun the man around, shoving his arm up behind his back.

The bully yelped and rose up on his tiptoes.

"Apologize to Ms. Amy," Sawyer said.

"The hell I will," Marion said.

Sawyer jacked his arm up higher.

"Fine," Marion gasped. "Sorry," he said as if spitting out the word.

"Say it nicely."

"Fuck you!"

Sawyer shoved the man's arm higher up the middle of his back. "Nicely."

The man was shaking with anger and pain. In a tightly controlled tone, through clenched teeth, Marion said, "I'm sorry, Amy."

Amy rubbed her arms. "Yeah. Well, don't do it again." She ducked past the big man in the white apron, standing in the swinging door to the kitchen.

"Bradshaw, you just treaded on my last nerve." The big guy marched across the diner to where Sawyer held Marion and took over.

Holding the man's arm up between his shoulder blades, the cook marched the bully toward the door. "Get the hell out of my diner and stay out. You're no longer welcome here." He shoved the man through the door, releasing him as he did.

Marion spun to face him. "I have just as much right to be here as anyone else."

The cook crossed his arms over his chest. "Not when you bully my waitresses. Now go, before I call the sheriff."

Marion smirked. "The sheriff and I go way back. He'll side with me."

"Yeah, well, we'll see." The cook pulled his cell-phone from his back pocket. "Yeah, Ms. Bippert, I need you to send a deputy…hell, send the sheriff over to the diner. Got Marion Bradshaw disturbing the peace. Thanks." The cook pulled a gun out of the back of his pants and held it lightly in his hands.

Marion's eyes narrowed. "You ain't gonna use that."

The cook lifted his chin. "Try me."

Marion straightened his shirt and sneered at the cook. "You serve lousy food. I don't need it." The man turned then mounted a motorcycle with skulls and flames painted across the tank. He started it, revved the engine and roared out of the parking lot, spinning up gravel in his wake.

CHAPTER 7

SAWYER WATCHED the motorcycle until it disappeared, then turned back to Kinsley.

She let go of a long, slow breath as if she'd been holding it throughout the altercation. She stood beside him, holding a glass jar of sugar in her grip like she wanted to use it as a weapon.

Sawyer's mouth twitched as he leaned close to her and extricated the jar from her fingers and set it on the table beside her. "Seems the show's over." He led her back to the table.

Moments later, Amy showed up with a carafe of coffee, her gaze on the window as if watching for Bradshaw's return. "Thank you for what you did."

Sawyer nodded.

"Marion's been an asshole to me since I went out with his son." Amy poured fresh coffee into Sawyer's cup, her hand quivering which made her spill a little. "If it's not hot enough for you, I'll get you a fresh cup."

"I'd rather you sat down for a few minutes with us," Sawyer said. "You're shaking."

She laughed, choking on the sound and sank into the seat opposite Sawyer and Kinsley.

Kinsley reached across the table and touched the girl's arm. "Are you okay?"

Amy stared down at where Kinsley's hand covered hers. "I'm not sure." She looked up into Kinsley's eyes. "I'm worried about Q."

"Q?" Kinsley gave her a quizzical glance.

"Quillen. His name seems so formal. He prefers to be called Q. He's also a big James Bond fan." She smiled, her eyes filling. "I haven't seen him in a few days. I'm afraid for him. Marion has always been too heavy-handed with him. I've seen him on days after his father has punched him in the face. He's come to me with black eyes, a busted lip and bruises all over." She lowered her voice and looked over her shoulder.

The other patrons had left after the fight with Marion. The diner was empty except for the cook, Amy and the other waitress.

"I begged him to leave his father. We could move to another state and start over. We wouldn't have much, but anything is better than what he's living with."

"Who is Marion Bradshaw?" Sawyer asked. "And why does he have people scared?"

Amy's lip curled back in a snarl. "He's the biggest bully in the county, and he's got a following. They call him Blade."

Sawyer's fist clenched. "Is he the leader of an organization called The Collective?"

Amy's eyes narrowed, and she slid toward the edge of the seat. "You with the DEA or DHS or some other government organization?"

"No," Sawyer said.

Kinsley shook her head and reached into her purse for the other sheet of paper she had with the image of her brother on it. "Actually, we're looking for this guy." She opened her mouth as if to say more, glanced over at Sawyer and closed her mouth again.

Sawyer wanted to smile at her restraint.

Now would not be a good time to reveal that she was Derek's sister, just in case Amy would tell her boyfriend Q. If she was dating the son of The Collective's leader, all bets were off on keeping secrets from them through her.

Amy stared at the photograph. For a second, Sawyer could swear the woman had a flash of recognition in her eyes. In the next moment, she looked up at Kinsley. "What do you want with him?"

"So, you've seen him?" Kinsley leaned forward. "Do you know where we can find him?"

"Is he in trouble with the law or something?" Amy asked. "Because, if he is, I'm not ratting anyone out. Unless it's Marion. In which case, I'd drive the bastard to jail myself."

"No, he's not in trouble with the law. We just want to find him," Kinsley said. "Please. Just tell me if you've seen him."

Amy looked from Kinsley to Sawyer and back, then shrugged. "Yeah. He was in town a couple of days ago with Q. I haven't seen either one of them since. And Q was supposed to take me out last Saturday. He stood me up." She stared out the window again. "I suspect Marion had something to do with that. I'm just wondering when Q will grow a pair of balls and stand up to that bastard. He swears his mother ran out on them when he was only eight years old. His dad is all he has." Amy snorted. "I'd be more likely to believe Marion killed her and buried her body in the mountains."

Sawyer wouldn't put it past the man. He was a sociopath, looking for a place to have a mental breakdown. Likely, he'd take as many down with him as he could.

"Amy, I could use some help in the kitchen if you're finished flapping your gums," Cookie called out from the kitchen door.

Amy jumped up. "I better get back to work. Cookie doesn't pay me unless I'm busy. He acts all tough, but the man's a teddy bear." She ran past the big man, smiling up at him. "Isn't that right?"

Cookie snorted. "Teddy bear? Not hardly." He patted his middle. "More like a grizzly."

After Amy disappeared into the kitchen, Cookie let the door swing shut behind her and crossed to where Sawyer and Kinsley sat and laid two plates in front of them with the food they'd ordered.

"You two better watch your backs," he warned. "Marion Bradshaw doesn't like to lose a fight. Everyone in town lets him get away with too much, just to keep the peace. Even Sheriff Parker lets him slide when he's doing dumb shit that's breaking minor laws."

Cookie nodded in the direction Bradshaw had gone. "Don't know what he's up to on that mountain, but it's bound to be no good. If you'd planned on staying the night in town, you might change your plans and find another town to sleep in tonight."

Sawyer tipped his head toward the older man. "Thanks for the warning. We hadn't planned on staying the night here." Sawyer frowned. "What about you? Are you safe?"

Cookie nodded. "I sleep with a loaded shotgun. And I advertise that fact."

"What about Amy?" Kinsley asked.

Cookie's brow wrinkled. "I'll have her stay with me and the missus tonight. Can't have one of my best waitresses quit on me because she's afraid of that jackass." The cook and owner of the diner, nodded toward the food on the table. "Your lunch is on the house. Thanks for rescuing Amy. She's a good kid. Too bad she's mixed up with the wrong guy."

"Q?" Kinsley asked.

"Quillen," Cookie corrected. "The boy isn't a bad kid. He didn't get to choose his parents. Or in his case, his father. He's just trying to survive." Cookie tapped a finger on the paper with Derek's photograph. "Saw Quillen with this kid a few days ago at the hardware store. Shame that he's mixed up with that bunch of radical idiots up on the mountain. They're all preparing for gloom and doom, stockpiling non-perishable foods, generators and ammunition. You'd think they were getting ready for the apocalypse."

"Is this guy up on that mountain?" Kinsley pointed to the photo of her brother.

"If he's with Quillen, he's up there," Cookie said. "Those two seemed like they were thick as thieves. Stuck together wherever they went in town. Yeah, I'd bet they're up on the mountain with Quillen's father, helping count the number of cans of vegetables and bags of beans they've collected from the grocery store. Can't buy any of that after they've gone through and cleared the shelves. Whatever. They're crazy as hell, and I have a diner to run." Cookie returned to the kitchen, leaving Sawyer and Kinsley to eat their lunch.

Sawyer packed away his sandwich and watched as Kinsley picked at hers.

"Aren't you going to eat that?" he asked.

She glanced up as if she'd forgotten he was there. "What? Oh." Her gaze went to the sandwich she'd pretty much destroyed. "I'm not hungry."

"If you're done, then we need to head back to the ranch."

Kinsley frowned. "And leave, knowing Derek is up there?"

"We can't go knocking on the door, demanding they release him."

Her frown deepened. "What if we take the sheriff? Can we get a warrant? Could we get onto that property with one?"

"I don't even think a warrant will get you past the guy manning the machinegun and that rifle-toting guard." Sawyer captured her gaze with his. "We need help. We have to go back and come up with a plan to extract your brother."

Kinsley sighed. "He's so close, I can feel it."

"Come on. Jake and Max will know how to get around that gate. They might know these mountains better than anyone and have a back door we can get through."

Kinsley's frown softened. "You think so?"

He wasn't sure of anything except that the two of them weren't enough to go up against The Collective.

They needed to back up, regroup and come up with a solid plan.

He almost laughed at his thought process. Of all people, he knew a plan never survived past the first encounter with the enemy. But having a plan was better than going in unprepared.

KINSLEY SAT QUIETLY on the trip back to Lost Valley Ranch, her mind back on that narrow road in the mountains. She'd been closer to her brother there than she'd been in a long time. And yet, she was still unable to see him, speak to him or reach out and touch him. She thought of her parents on their cruise completely unaware that their only son was in such a dangerous situation.

If Kinsley had her way, they wouldn't know about it until she got Derek safely away from Bradshaw and his stupid group. But it wouldn't hurt to let RJ and Gunny know that, if anything happened to her and her brother, to notify her parents. She'd have to leave information with them for just such an occurrence.

She lifted her chin and stared out at the waning light. The mountains robbed Fool's Gold of an extra thirty minutes of light by casting them in shadow when the sun ducked below the peaks.

Part of Kinsley wished they could collect the other members of the Brotherhood Protectors and hurry back to rescue her brother. But Sawyer was right. They couldn't go barreling into The Collective's compound without knowing a little about what they were up against.

Jake and Max stepped out on the porch as Sawyer pulled up in front of the lodge.

Kinsley didn't wait for Sawyer to round the front of the truck to open her door. As soon as he parked, she dropped down out of her seat onto the ground and met Sawyer at the front of the vehicle. She took his hand and held it as they approached the lodge and his new boss.

"Any luck?" Jake asked.

Sawyer nodded. "We think we know about where Kinsley's brother is."

"About?"

Sawyer nodded. "Let's take this into the basement. I assume you can bring up maps on the big screen?"

"You bet." Jake led the way through the lodge to the basement door in the kitchen. As soon as they started down the stairs, the lights blinked on.

Kinsley followed, amazed at how modern the Colorado division of the Brotherhood Protectors headquarters appeared. A large conference table took up one corner of the space with a huge screen at the end.

Max crossed to a computer keyboard, booted the system, then clicked several keys until the big screen blinked to life and a map appeared displaying Pikes

Peak and the surrounding towns and roads within a hundred miles.

Between Sawyer and Kinsley, they homed in on the location where they'd been threatened by the guards at the gate to The Collective's current compound. The guys studied a contour map that showed the elevations of the area surrounding the gate. They switched back and forth between the contour map and a satellite map that showed a group of buildings at the end of the road the gate had blocked.

After an hour in discussion over the best way to get to those buildings without going through the gate, Kinsley bailed.

Exhausted from the stress of the day, she climbed the stairs to the kitchen where she found RJ making a pot of homemade hot cocoa.

Without asking, she poured a mug full and handed it to Kinsley.

RJ held up a bag. "Marshmallows?"

Kinsley reached into the bag and grabbed a handful, dropping them into the steaming chocolate milk, and then sipped carefully. The hot liquid warmed a path all the way down to her belly.

"Thanks," she said. "I needed that."

"I hear you might have found your brother's location," RJ said.

Kinsley nodded. "We think so. Now, they're trying to figure out how to get to him and bring him out."

"And you're wishing you could just go now and get him."

"How did you guess?"

"That's what I'd want to do. I can be a little impatient when I want things to happen. And I don't like being dependent on others to get things done."

Kinsley grinned over the rim of her mug. "Exactly."

"You should know, they have yours and your brother's best interests at heart," RJ said.

Kinsley sighed. "I know."

"And they're highly trained at this kind of thing. You couldn't ask for better. If anyone can get him out, they can. They've done this kind of thing before."

"I know. But it's so hard to stand by and do nothing."

"If you want something to do, I can put you to work tomorrow here at the ranch?" RJ said with a grin. "Take your pick. You can help in the lodge or muck horse stalls."

Kinsley laughed. "I could use the distraction. But I wouldn't know the first thing about horses, having grown up in the city."

"Lodge, it is," RJ said. "There's always laundry, making beds, dusting or dishes."

"I can do any of those things, as long as the guys don't need me." She glanced toward the door to the basement.

"Trust me, they'll want you out of their way. You'll be a distraction otherwise."

Kinsley held up her hands. "Trust me, I don't want to get in the way of them rescuing Derek. He's my only sibling."

RJ sighed. "You're lucky to have him. I grew up an only child. I always wanted a brother." She grinned. "Now I have a couple in Max and Cage Weaver. You haven't met him yet, but you will. And I'm sure Sawyer will be the same once he gets used to us. When they join the brotherhood, they became part of the family here at Lost Valley Ranch."

"You love it here, don't you?"

RJ nodded. "I tried to join the army right out of high school, but a medical condition kept them from letting me in. I've been here on the ranch since, helping Gunny manage this crazy, nutty place and the Watering Hole. I didn't think life could get better until the Brotherhood Protectors asked to use our basement as their headquarters. Then I met Jake." RJ's face softened. "Life only got better."

Kinsley glanced again at the door to the basement, half-wishing Sawyer would come up. She'd like to see him again before she called it a night. But no one emerged, and she was down to her last sip of cocoa and one last marshmallow. "I guess I'd better get my shower and go to bed. Hopefully, the guys will fill me in tomorrow."

"Most likely," RJ said. "Let me know if you need anything."

"Thanks for the cocoa." Kinsley rinsed her cup and placed it in the dishwasher. Then she climbed the stairs, grabbed her toiletries and headed for the bathroom.

After her shower, the room beside hers was still empty.

She entered her room, closed the door and paced. The walls seemed to close in around her. Wrapping a blanket around her shoulders, she stepped out onto the balcony and drew in a deep breath of the cool night air.

It helped. But what she really wanted was to see Sawyer one more time before she tried to sleep. He'd been the steady influence in her life since she'd boarded that plane in Denver.

She worried that she was becoming too dependent on him in her life. When they got her brother out, she'd have to move on, find a job and get on with living.

Until then, she wouldn't pass up a moment with Sawyer. He was everything she could ever imagine wanting in a man. Maybe, when this was over, he'd consider taking her out on a date.

Oh, she'd like that. A lot. Hell, she might even invite him into her bed.

The thought of lying naked with Sawyer rushed into her thoughts, making her body hot with desire.

A desire hotter than anything she'd ever felt with the doctor.

But then, the doctor hadn't been as tall, dark and handsome as Sawyer. And the doctor hadn't treated her with as much care and consideration as Sawyer.

What she wouldn't give to be held by Sawyer at that moment. Yeah, and he'd think she was needy or something. Well, wasn't she?

CHAPTER 8

AFTER AN HOUR and a half in the basement with Max and Jake planning their route into the compound, coupled with the stress of the day, Sawyer was ready to call it a night.

One other member of the team would be there early in the morning to be briefed on the operation prior to them leaving for the mountain. They'd go in and recon the area, then lie low until dark, sneak in, find Kinsley's brother and get him out without waking everyone else.

Easy.

Sawyer snorted. In his experience, nothing was ever as easy as the plans they made prior to a mission. But without a plan, things were twice as likely to go wrong.

The men left the basement and retired to their rooms upstairs.

Sawyer hurried through his shower and crossed the hallway, pausing in front of Kinsley's room. He pressed his ear to the door but didn't hear any sounds from within. She'd probably gone to sleep.

He sighed, entered his room, turned off the light and lay on his bed. After several minutes with his eyes wide open and his thoughts racing, he left his bed and stepped out onto the balcony.

A movement to his left caught his eye. He turned to discover someone leaning against the rail, wrapped in a blanket.

When she turned her face toward him, the starlight shone down on her face and filled him with a longing so strong, it nearly brought him to his knees.

"Hey," he said and closed the distance between him and Kinsley. "Can't sleep?"

She shook her head. "You?"

He shook his head. "Need a hug?" What made him ask that, he didn't know. No. He knew. It was what was in his own heart. He needed a hug. From her.

"Yes," she whispered, stepped into his one-armed embrace and leaned her cheek against his chest. "I needed this. I needed you." Her voice faded off. If the night had not been so silent, he might not have heard her words.

"I needed this and needed you, too." He leaned his cheek against her damp hair.

"You're strong and capable," she said. "Why do you need me?"

He chuckled. "You remind me why I lived when my buddies didn't. For a long time, I resented that I was spared when two of my friends weren't. They were more deserving of life. They had wives. One of them had a baby on the way. Why did they have to die when I didn't have anyone waiting for me back home?"

Kinsley rested her hands on his chest and leaned back to stare up at him. "Your life is worth so much. You can't beat yourself up over something you had no control over."

"Easier to say than to do. But you remind me why I lived. I still have purpose in my life. Right now, it's to help you."

She reached up and touched his cheek with the palm of her hand. "I hope that's not the only purpose you have for living," she said softly.

"It's not. But it's a start." He turned his face and pressed his lips to the palm of her hand.

"I think you have more purpose than helping me."

"Like?" he asked as he pressed his lips to her forehead.

"Like kissing me," she said, her voice light and breathy.

He lowered his face until his mouth hovered over hers. "My purpose is to kiss you?"

She nodded and then lifted up on her toes, to close the distance.

As their lips touched, Sawyer's body ignited. His arm tightened around her back, crushing her to him as he drank in her taste, her scent and the feel of her body pressed to his. It was heaven.

And he wanted so much more.

Kinsley's hands reached up to encircle the back of his neck, urging him to go deeper. She opened to him, and his tongue swept in to claim hers.

A moan rose up her throat, and her body melted against his.

They were so close. But not close enough.

As the kiss deepened, she lowered her hands and slipped them beneath his T-shirt, skimming lightly across his skin, rising up to find and tweak the tight little nipples on his chest.

Sawyer groaned into her mouth. In the past, when he was whole, he would have scooped her into his arms and carried her into the bedroom where he would have stripped her naked and made sweet love to her.

His limp arm put a damper on his desire, reminding him of his limitations.

Kinsley didn't seem to recognize any such thing. She pushed the T-shirt up over his head.

Sawyer slipped his good arm out of it, and she dragged the rest over his useless one. Then she kissed his left shoulder and trailed kisses down to the hand that had no feeling.

He started to pull away, but she wouldn't let him. "This is who you are now," she said. "It doesn't scare me. It makes me appreciate you even more." She lifted his left hand and rested his palm against her cheek. "You gave so much of yourself for your country and your brothers in arms. It's who you are." She lowered his hand to his side and let the blanket around her shoulders fall to the decking. She wore only a filmy white nightgown. When she stood with her back to the starlight, her shape was silhouetted beneath it.

Kinsley took his right hand and led him into her bedroom.

Sawyer's pulse sped as he pulled his hand free and closed the French door behind them.

When he turned back to Kinsley, she had her hands on the hem of her nightgown. Her gaze captured his as she raised the hem up over her hips, exposing a pair of lacy white bikini panties that hugged her slender hips and barely covered her sex.

His heart lodged in his throat, Sawyer drank in every detail of her perfect body as the nightgown rose upward.

When the gown cleared her head, she tossed it onto a chair in the corner and stood before him barefooted, wearing nothing but the panties and a secret smile.

"You don't have to do this," he felt compelled to say.

Her brow wrinkled. "Don't you want me?"

"Sweet Jesus, yes. But if this is a pity fuck, I don't." His chest tightened.

Kinsley laughed. "All the while I dated the doctor, I never wanted to strip his clothes off him and make crazy, mad, hot sex with him." She took a step forward. "Right here. Right now. I want to do that with you more than anything." She took another step in his direction, coming to stand less than a foot away, her breasts within easy reach...taunting... tempting. "Are you with me?"

He leaned his head back, counted to three to tamp down the surge of desire claiming every cell in his body. Then he opened his eyes and looked directly into hers. "I want you more than I've ever wanted a woman in my life. And frankly, that scares me."

She chuckled. "You? Scared?" Her hand rose to rest on his chest, and then moved down his torso, past his bellybutton to the waistband of his jeans. "You're a Navy SEAL. They're not afraid of anything, right?"

He captured her hand in his. "I'm afraid of disappointing you. I'm not the man I used to be. I haven't...made love since...well, before I lost the use of my left forearm. I'm not even sure I can." His words seemed to echo in the quiet of her room.

He'd just admitted he wasn't sure he could get his manhood to perform. What if it was broken, too?

"We'll just have to find your limits." She shook her hand free of his, flicked the button on his jeans open and slid the zipper down.

His cock sprang free, hard and thick.

She took it in her hands and caressed his length from tip to base, pausing to fondle his balls. "I think you're okay in this department. But you might need further proof to boost your confidence." She knelt on the floor and touched her tongue to his velvety head and traced the rim all the way around.

Sawyer's body tensed. He reached out to capture her hair in his hand and urged her to continue.

"Like that?"

"Hell yeah," he said on a gasp.

"I'm thinking your parts are in working order," she said and slid her mouth over his cock, taking him in as far as she could go until he bumped against the back of her throat. At the same time, she cupped him, stroking his balls, making the fire in his veins burn white-hot.

Then she leaned back, letting him slide almost all the way out of her. After flicking his tip with her tongue, she gripped his buttock and pulled him back into her, settling into a steady rhythm in and out, her fingers on his ass digging in with each thrust.

As the sensations mounted, his body stiffened. He was so close to release he could barely suck air into his lungs. When he thought he might explode, he pulled free and dragged in huge, gulping breaths. Then he gripped her arm and backed her toward the bed until she bumped against it and sat on the edge.

"Your turn," he said.

"You don't have to." Her words echoed his.

Sawyer smiled. "Yes, I do. If I want you to come, calling out my name, I have to bring you to the edge. There's only one way to be certain I will." He smiled and dropped to his knees, parted her legs and moved in to claim her.

First, he hooked his finger in the elastic band of her panties and dragged them down and off her legs, tossing them over his shoulder. Then he draped her legs over his shoulders, parted her folds and flicked the little nubbin hidden at the top.

Kinsley's legs tightened around his ears. She fell back against the bed and ran her hands over her flat belly.

As he flicked, licked and nibbled on that sensitive spot, she bucked and moaned in response.

His body reacted in kind, his cock becoming impossibly hard.

The more he took her with his mouth, the more she writhed until she suddenly went still, her body tightening all over, her hips pulsing ever so slightly.

She clamped her eyes shut and dug her nails into his shoulders as she strained to milk her release for all it was worth. When at last she settled back against the mattress, her arms fell to her sides, and she chuckled. "Wow."

"Wow, good?" he asked as he tongued her there one more time before pushing to his feet.

Kinsley stared up at him, her face flushed, a smile curving the corners of her mouth. "Not good," she said.

His heart nose-dived into his belly.

"Not good." Kinsley grinned. "Great!"

He reached for his jeans, removed his wallet and pulled out a small, foil packet.

"Let me," Kinsley held out her hand.

"I've got this," he said as he tore the foil open with his teeth and held the packet in his mouth to dig out the condom. Then he placed it over the tip of his shaft and expertly started rolling it down his length.

Kinsley came up on an elbow and took over to finish cloaking him, holding him a moment longer in her grip.

With her gaze locked with his, she guided him to her entrance.

Sawyer touched her there, poised to enter, loving how wanton she looked lying against the quilt, her auburn hair splayed out across the mattress like a burnished fan.

His control slipped, and he drove into her, holding her left hip for leverage as he thrust deep, again and again.

Sawyer had worried he wouldn't be able to pleasure her the way she'd pleasured him. He'd been afraid he wouldn't be able to remain hard throughout their lovemaking. He'd been worried for nothing. The woman inspired him to do more, harder and faster.

Kinsley gripped the backs of her thighs and pulled them up, giving Sawyer a better angle to drive even deeper. She threw back her head and lifted her hips to meet his every thrust.

As the tension mounted inside, Sawyer sent a silent prayer to the heavens for sparing his masculinity. Then he drove deep one last time, buried inside her as he spent his release. His shaft throbbed and pulsed against the walls of her channel.

For a long moment, she remained still, holding her thighs, her legs spread wide.

With the waves of sensation waning, Sawyer slipped free of her.

Kinsley scooted up on the bed and laid her head on the pillow.

Sawyer settled on the bed beside her, lying on his left side. He wrapped his right arm around her and spooned her back to his front.

He nibbled her earlobe and whispered, "You are amazing."

She leaned against him, reaching back to cup his buttocks in her hand. "You're not bad yourself."

"Thank you," he whispered.

She laughed. "You don't have to thank me. it's not like I fetched you a cup of water."

"It is, in a way," he said, his voice hoarse. "When I thought my well was empty for good, you filled it."

Her hand tightened on his ass for a moment. Then she turned beneath his arm to face him. "You have so much more to give in this life. Don't sell yourself short. Even with only one arm..." she leaned into him and brushed her lips across his, "you're more of a man than most I've met. If I'm not very careful...I could fall for a guy like you."

His heart swelled with hope for the future. One that just might include this incredible woman he'd known such a short time. But didn't she deserve a better man then him? He frowned, pushing that thought to the back of his mind as he held her naked body pressed to his. "Sleep, sweetheart. You might feel differently in the morning."

She shook her head and rested her cheek against his chest. "I doubt it," she said, her voice barely a whisper. "You can't change who you are, and I can't change the way I feel."

When he started to argue, she pressed a finger to his lips. "Don't overthink this. Just accept it, for now." She drew in a deep breath and let it out on a sigh as she closed her eyes.

He lay still, listening to the sound of her steady breathing, taking it all in. The musky scent of their lovemaking, the warmth of her body and the silky smoothness of her skin against his.

She fought fiercely for her family and had challenged her fear of heights in an airplane and on the edge of a cliff to find out what had happened to her brother. Kinsley was the whole package, inside and out.

Sawyer could get used to making love to her every night and waking beside her in the early morning light. He could easily fall in love with her. Or was he infatuated with the first woman who hadn't judged him for the invalid he'd become?

He closed his eyes and repeated to himself. *Don't overthink everything.*

CHAPTER 9

KINSLEY SLEPT DEEPLY without dreams or nightmares. When she woke, she had to remember where she was.

As the previous night rushed back in on her, she turned over and stared at the empty pillow beside her. It still had the indentation from Sawyer's head.

She sat up, realizing she was still naked from making love to the man. Never in the time she'd been with her ex, Jason, had she slept naked throughout the night. After making love, they'd risen, showered and dressed in pajamas in case the apartment building caught on fire. Not once in their relationship had the building gone up in flames. The same could be said of sex with Jason. It hadn't been anything more than blah.

Kinsley snagged her toiletries, wrapped a robe around her body and ducked across the hallway into the bathroom. After a quick shower, she dressed in jeans, a white T-shirt and tennis shoes. She braided her damp hair into a thick ponytail that hung down her back. If she had to go into battle, at least her hair would be out of her face.

Hopefully, she wouldn't have to. The men of the Brotherhood Protectors had the necessary skills to accomplish the mission of extracting her brother from a hostile camp. They'd all stated it was a common mission they'd performed on numerous occasions while on active duty.

But how different was active duty to operating in a civilian world with its own set of rules?

Rather than pace inside her room, going through every imaginable scenario, Kinsley descended the stairs and made her way to the kitchen.

As she passed through the dining room, she noted several tables filled with guests. A couple in their late sixties or early seventies were just finishing breakfast. A family of four sat around another table, the kids eating cereal, the adults enjoying Gunny's omelets, bacon and toast.

Kinsley's stomach rumbled at the scent of bacon emanating from the kitchen. She pushed through the swinging door to find Gunny pushing scrambled eggs around a skillet and RJ elbow-deep in a sink full of soap suds.

"About time you showed up," Gunny said. "We were beginning to think you'd left with the others."

Kinsley frowned. "They left already?" She glanced at the clock on the wall over the stove. It wasn't even seven o'clock.

"They left before dawn," Gunny said. "They wanted to get up the mountain before people in the compound started moving around. The fewer people who see them, the better."

RJ rinsed a pan and dried it off. After wiping her hands on the towel, she hung it on a hook on the wall. "They'll find your brother."

Kinsley gave the other woman a weak smile. "I know they will. But it's hard to stand back and do nothing."

"Have some scrambled eggs and bacon," Gunny said. "Good food will help take your mind off your worries."

"Then you can help me change the bed linens and clean the bathrooms." RJ winked. "Seriously, you don't have to do all that. JoJo will be here shortly. She helps out between the lodge and the

bar. And she fixes things that break, like tractors and four-wheelers."

"What does JoJo stand for?" Kinsley asked.

RJ grinned. "Josephina Angelica Barrera-Ramirez. But she never answers to that. We've been friends since high school. Other than her four-year stint in the Army, she's been here, working for Lost Valley Ranch."

The swinging door blasted inward and a petite

woman with dark brown hair and brown-black eyes breezed in followed by a medium-sized dog with short, yellow fur, one perky ear and one floppy one.

"Buenas dias." The whirlwind of a tiny woman stopped to give Gunny a peck on the cheek. "How's my favorite jarhead Marine?"

"Good. And how's my favorite Army grunt?" He scooped eggs from the pan onto a plate and added a piece of bacon and a slice of buttered toast. Gathering up the offering, he turned to JoJo. "Sit down and eat breakfast with Ms. Brothers."

Kinsley smile at the other woman. "Please. I'd like the company. And you can tell me how you and RJ became friends."

JoJo turned her attention to Kinsley. "RJ and I go way back. Even before that time when I became Gunny's spare daughter." She winked toward Gunny. "He adopted me when I was a senior in high school. Well, he didn't really adopt me, but he took me in and gave me a place to stay to finish out school when I had nowhere else to go."

RJ smirked. "It's what he does."

Gunny pulled a tray of lemon poppyseed muffins out of the oven and set it on the stovetop. When he straightened, he shot a frown toward RJ. "What do I do?"

"Collect strays!" RJ and JoJo exclaimed at the same time and laughed.

"I don't collect strays. I take them to the shelters."

"Not stray animals," RJ said. "You collect stray people. Folks who need help but don't have the resources."

"Like me," JoJo said, "when my folks up and died while I was still a kid in high school, you gave me a home."

"And then there's Emily Strayhorn, one of the nicest people you'll ever meet," RJ said. "You gave her a place to stay for free while she continued her education and got her psychology degree, masters and doctorate."

Gunny shrugged. "I didn't do much."

RJ snorted. "The hell you didn't. You gave those women what they needed to get on with their lives, never asking for anything in return."

"And they're giving back," Gunny retorted. He tipped his chin toward JoJo. "You gave time in service to your country, and now, your community. Emily works with veterans, helping them cope with shit they can't deal with on a daily basis. I'd say they're giving back."

"Now, you're providing a place for the Brotherhood Protectors to operate out of Colorado." RJ hugged her father. "You're a good man, Gunny."

"You're ruining my image of being a badass jarhead." He snorted. "Besides, the brotherhood pays the rent, and they saved my daughter when she needed help." He hugged her back. "For that, they could stay for free. But don't tell them that. It takes a lot of cash to keep this place running."

Gunny filled another plate full of fluffy yellow scrambled eggs, bacon and toast and handed it to Kinsley. "Go with JoJo and eat at a table in the dining room. RJ and I will join you in a minute. I could use a cup of coffee before I head to town for supplies."

"You know, I could make that run for you," RJ volunteered.

Gunny shook his head. "I'd let you, but I have a doctor's appointment at the VA hospital to renew my prescriptions. Then I'll swing by the feed store and grocery store for provisions. You'll have to hold down the fort while I'm out. If you need me, leave a text message. I don't always get good reception inside the VA or I might be in the middle of my screening."

"We gotcha covered," RJ said. "JoJo and I can handle everything."

"I can only be here for an hour," JoJo said. "I have to take Roscoe to the vet for his annual checkup. I'll be back after that to finish up around here and man the Watering Hole for the lunch crowd."

"Sounds like a plan." RJ reached down and scratched behind the dog's ear. "Don't go flirting with the other dogs while you're there." She grinned across at Kinsley. "Roscoe is a lover. He loves everyone and every dog. Sometimes, a little too much."

The dog looked up and appeared to be smiling with his tongue hanging out.

RJ shook her head. "He's the only dog I know who likes going to the vet."

JoJo grinned and patted the dog's head. "They give him treats. He remembers going hungry in Afghanistan. He loves anyone who gives him food. If I left food down for him, he'd be a fat boy."

Kinsley balanced her plate in one hand and bent to scratch behind Roscoe's floppy ear. "You are a lover, aren't you?"

"Watch him," JoJo warned. "He's also a thief. He'll have that food off your plate before you even know he's been there."

Kinsley laughed and followed JoJo into the dining room where she settled her plate on a table designated for the staff of the Lost Valley Ranch.

Kinsley laid her plate on the opposite side of the table from JoJo, feeling a little awkward with this new person.

"I hear you're looking for your brother around the Cripple Creek area," JoJo said as she settled into her chair.

"I am."

"Max says you're moving out here to keep an eye on him after you get him free of the people who have him."

Kinsley nodded. "If he decides to stay."

"And if it's safe to stay once you liberate him." JoJo

stared across the table at Kinsley. "The Collective might take issue with having one of their own taken. Your brother might know some of the secrets that group is harboring. They might kill him to keep him from telling all."

Kinsley's hand fumbled with her fork, and she dropped it. The utensil clattered against the plate.

JoJo's brow furrowed. "Sorry. I didn't mean to upset you."

"No," Kinsley said. "That's just one of the scenarios that has gone through my head since we learned he was with The Collective. I just can't let that happen. He's my brother. The only brother I have. As his big sister, I practically raised him." Her voice hitched as a sob rose up her throat to block her vocal cords.

JoJo reached across the table to cover her hand. "The Brotherhood Protectors will come through for you. And they'll protect your brother with their lives."

The thought of Sawyer sacrificing himself to save her brother didn't make Kinsley feel any better. She liked the man and could easily fall in love with him. Hadn't he sacrificed enough already?

Gunny and RJ joined them, each carrying a cup of coffee.

The conversation went to what needed to be done that day in the lodge and the barn. Gunny briefed

JoJo on changes he'd made in the bar next door and where he'd stored certain supplies.

Though the four members of the Brotherhood Protectors were out conducting a reconnaissance mission into a hostile compound, life went on at the Lost Valley Ranch.

To Kinsley, it was surreal. Her thoughts and her heart were with the men and her brother. Talking about rooms that needed cleaning and stalls to be mucked seemed so inconsequential. And yet, necessary to keep her grounded.

When JoJo finished her breakfast, she pushed back from the table and carried her plate into the kitchen. Kinsley followed, having barely touched her own food. She couldn't. Her stomach roiled at the thought of Sawyer and his team in danger of being shot by the gun-crazy men guarding the compound.

"I'll take care of the dishes," Gunny said. "If you don't mind helping out, you can get started with RJ upstairs. I'm heading out as soon as I wrap up things in the kitchen and make my list of needed supplies."

Kinsley left the kitchen and found RJ carrying a load of sheets and towels out of a room on the main level.

"There are more sheets and towels in the laundry room. Grab a stack and come on up."

Kinsley found the laundry room and a neat stack of sheets and towels on a folding table. She carried them up to the second floor where RJ showed her which rooms and bathrooms needed to be cleaned, have towels replaced and beds in need of changing.

The work was simple and didn't require her to think too hard. Which left her with too much room in her head to worry about what was happening on that mountain. She wished she could have gone with them. However, if she had, Sawyer might have been distracted by the need to protect her. She wanted him to have full focus on recovering her brother, without getting injured in the process.

Several times during the hour, she checked her cellphone. Not that Sawyer would call her from where they were going. Reception had been spotty to non-existent with all that solid rock surrounding the camp. She wouldn't know anything until they came down off that mountain.

Still, she was so far away from what was happening. Surely, if she was in Cripple Creek, she'd be in a better position to help.

She snorted as she fit a pillow into a clean pillowcase.

Help with what? She wasn't familiar with shooting guns. The roads in the mountain were treacherous, and she was afraid of heights. What good would she be?

She checked her cellphone again, sighed and slipped it into her back pocket.

As she propped the pillow against the headboard, her cellphone rang and vibrated against her backside.

Her heart leaped into her throat as she grabbed for the device and held it up to read the caller ID.

DEREK BROTHERS

KINSLEY'S BREATH caught in her throat. She'd watched for weeks for that name to pop up on her screen. In her hurry to answer, she stabbed at the screen.

"Derek!" she cried.

"Kinsley Brothers," a familiar voice said into her ear. She knew that voice, having heard the man harassing the waitress in Cookie's Cripple Creek diner. "If you want to see your brother, be at the Fool's Gold ghost town saloon in one hour. If you don't show, or you come with anyone else, you'll never see your brother alive again. Involve the law, and he'll die a painful death."

Kinsley swallowed hard, forcing calm in her words. "How do I know he isn't already dead?"

A moment of silence was followed by the crackling of plastic hitting a hard surface as if someone dropped the cellphone.

"Kinsley!" Derek's sweet voice sounded in Kinsley's ear.

She fell to her knees, tears welling in her eyes. He was alive! "Derek, sweetie. Are you all right?"

"Don't do what he wants. Stay away from these

people!" His voice faded as if he were being dragged away.

"Derek!" Kinsley staggered to her feet as if she could go where they were taking him.

"Be there," Bradshaw commanded.

"Only if you bring my brother," she said through the tears streaming down her face. "If I don't see my brother, I leave." She'd seen the touristy ghost town. There would be people milling about even during the off-season. Someone would see them. Surely, if she called out, they'd help.

"Kinsley?" RJ said from the door to the room she'd been working. "What's wrong?"

Kinsley turned toward the other woman. She held out her hand holding her cellphone. More tears welled in her eyes. "Derek."

RJ's face lit with a smile. She crossed the room to stand in front of Kinsley. "He called?" Her smile faded and a frown dented her forehead. "Is he okay?"

"I don't know. It was Blade, the leader of The Collective." Her tears slipped silently down her face. "He wants me to meet him in an hour, or he'll kill Derek."

"I'm calling the sheriff." RJ yanked her cellphone from her pocket.

Kinsley placed her hand over RJ's phone. "No. He told me not to bring anyone. And that, if I involve the law, he'd make Derek's death painful." The more she thought about the threats, the drier her eyes became. "The bastard is using my brother to get to me."

"Why does he want you?" RJ asked.

Kinsley paced across the room, her head down, thinking. "We embarrassed him at the diner in Cripple Creek. Maybe he's using me to lure Sawyer to him as retribution." She stopped and looked across the room at RJ. "He's already got Derek. I can't let him take Sawyer as well."

"Maybe he knows the guys are out there, and they want you as a bargaining chip." RJ frowned heavily. "We need to let the men know what's happening." She raised her cellphone and dialed a number. After a few moments, she lowered her hand. "No response."

"There is no cellphone reception up on that mountain," Kinsley said. "They won't know what's happening until they come back down."

"You can't meet Blade alone."

"I told him I would leave if I didn't see my brother."

"That's *if* he lets you leave," RJ said.

"That ghost town had people on the streets when I drove by yesterday."

"It usually does. Why would he meet you during the middle of the day?"

"Maybe he wants to use those people as human shields." Kinsley shook her head. "No matter what, I have to go. If I don't, he'll hurt or kill my brother."

"I'm not letting you go alone," RJ said. "JoJo just left. Let me see if I can get her on the phone."

"No," Kinsley said. "He was adamant that I arrive alone."

"So, you arrive alone. We'll go in separate vehicles. JoJo and I'll be another couple of tourists."

Kinsley's eyes narrowed. "You don't think he'll recognize you or JoJo?"

"Not if we wear hats and dress like we're out to buy Colorado trinkets and take pictures of the fake storefronts."

"Okay. But whatever you do, don't let them know you're with me."

"What's your plan? You don't think they'll just let Derek go, do you?"

"No, but if I don't show up, they might follow through on their threat. I couldn't live with myself, if, by not being there, my brother dies."

RJ's lips pressed together, and she stared down at her cellphone. "We really need to let the guys know what's going on." She looked up. "At the very least, we should let Hank Patterson know what's happening."

"What good will that do? He's in Montana. He couldn't get here in an hour, even if he had a plane at his disposal."

RJ grinned. "Actually, I think he does. And in the meantime, he might have some suggestions as to how to handle the situation."

Kinsley glanced down at the clock on her cellphone. "I now have fifty-five minutes. If we're going to talk to Hank, we need to do it as we move."

The women ran down the stairs and across the great room and dining room. RJ hit the swinging door and held it for Kinsley to pass through. She raced to the door leading down to the basement, pressed her thumb to the pad and waited for the biometrics to unlock the door.

She gave Kinsley a crooked smile. "I'm an honorary member of the brotherhood. Not only that, we own the building." Leading the way down, she crossed to the computer terminal in a corner that had an array of monitors mounted on the wall.

When she barely touched the mouse, the screens all blinked to life.

"Now, to remember how to bring Hank up on video conferencing." She looked around the desk. "I know there were instructions here somewhere." Her hand landed on a laminated card, and she grinned. "Ah. Here it is."

Kinsley leaned over her shoulder and read the instructions as RJ tapped the keys on the keyboard. The sound of a phone ringing made her glance up. "Fingers crossed," she whispered.

A big man with white-blond hair appeared on the middle monitor.

"RJ, what's up?"

"Hey, Swede." RJ tipped her head toward Kinsley. "We have a situation." She explained about the call

Kinsley had received, the threats and the fact the men were all out on reconnaissance, out of communication with the ranch.

Swede hit the keyboard in front of him, typing madly. "I just sent a text to Hank. He's in LA with Sadie and the kids. He'll get back to me as soon as he can. I've also notified our team here in Montana. Anyone who isn't currently assigned is to report to the landing strip on the ranch here. I have a pilot on standby, ready to fly here, pick up our guys and head your way."

"See?" RJ smiled at Kinsley. "I told you they had access to a plane."

"Yeah, but we might not be there in time for your meeting," Swede said. "I believe there's a small landing strip on the edge of Fool's Gold."

"JoJo and I will drop a vehicle off there for your team to use," RJ said.

Swede dipped his head. "In the meantime, if you're dead set on meeting up with that guy, take one of the GPS tracking discs that looks like a necklace. Jake should have a stash of them in the communications room."

Kinsley pulled the necklace out of her shirt and held it up. "Like this one?" Sawyer had given it to her the night they'd arrived at the ranch, explaining how it was used.

Swede nodded. "I see Jake and Sawyer have you covered. Are you familiar with firing a pistol?"

Kinsley shook her head.

Swede's lips pressed together. "Then don't take a gun. You might hurt yourself or give them just one more way to kill you. Check in the arms room for a knife. Find one you can hide on your person. More than likely, they'll search you for a weapon. I know Hank likes to keep some knives that can make it past a metal detector. You'll need something slim, sharp and that can't be discovered during a pat-down. You'll need something like that in case they tie you up with rope, zip-ties or duct tape."

"You're scaring me," Kinsley muttered.

"Trust me," he said. "I'm scared *for* you. This guy Blade has a nasty reputation for having a hair-trigger temper."

"I've witnessed it." Kinsley pushed a hand through her hair. "He's a Class-A jerk, and he bullies people. He even has the sheriff tiptoeing around him. Which I don't' get." She glanced at her cellphone clock. "I have fifty minutes to be where I need to be. I don't suppose you can teach me self-defense in that short a timeframe."

Swede shook his head. "I wish I was there. I'd go with you."

"Can't," Kinsley. "He said I had to come alone."

"There are ways to work around that."

"I'm not letting her go alone," RJ said. "JoJo and I will be there, if only for moral support. And we'll follow them wherever they go."

"Bradshaw is a trained Marine," Swede said. "He'll know to have backup. Look out for them. He might be counting on someone tagging along. You might be caught right along with Kinsley."

"We'll be careful," RJ insisted. "I can't let her go in there alone."

"You have to. At least into the saloon," Kinsley said.

"I wish you had a little more time," Swede said. "I'd like our guys to be in place before you meet with Bradshaw."

"I'm not calling the shots." Kinsley was just a pawn in whatever game Bradshaw was playing.

Swede continued. "Get some headsets out of the communications room so you can talk to each other as the scene plays out. RJ, you know what to get…?"

"I think I can figure it out," RJ said.

"Ladies, I wish I could be there for you," Swede said, a frown pushing his eyebrows together. "I'm glad you let us know what's going on. If they take you, at least we'll have a way to find you."

RJ ended the video call.

Kinsley squared her shoulders and turned to RJ. "We only have a few minutes to figure this all out before I have to leave to get to town on time. Let's do this."

"Right." RJ clapped her hands together. "JoJo is on her way back from the vet's office. We can bring her up to speed when she arrives. Let's get the radio headsets out and tested. We can use our hair to hide the fact we'll be wearing them." She led the way to a room where an array of electronic devices lined the shelves. She opened a drawer, pulled out three sets of earbuds and handed one to Kinsley. She fit one set in her ears as Kinsley did the same, and then tested for sound. "Testing, testing."

"I hear you," Kinsley said. "Can you hear me?"

RJ nodded. "Loud and clear." She inserted the other set intended for JoJo's use in her ears and made certain they could hear each other through them as well. Moving to another drawer, she fished out a hand-held device, switched it on and stared down at a little screen. Four green dots appeared on a map.

"Each one of the Brotherhood Protectors' women carries one of the necklaces like yours." RJ pointed to three grouped closer together. "These three are you, me and JoJo." She pointed to the one farther away. "That would be Emily. She works in Colorado Springs at the VA hospital. We can track you if we get separated." Clipping the device to her belt, she closed the drawers and left the room.

Kinsley followed her into the next room where guns of all shapes and sizes lined the walls.

RJ took one of the handguns, a magazine filled with bullets and a shoulder holster. She slipped the shoulder holster over her arms and buckled it across her chest, the slid the handgun into the leather pocket.

"You know how to use that?" Kinsley asked.

RJ nodded. "My father was a Marine. He raised me to be able to protect myself."

Kinsley sighed. "I led a very sheltered life in Savannah."

"I can show you how to shoot when this is all over. Now isn't the time to learn. They'll just take the weapon off you and use it against you or someone else."

"That's what I'm afraid of."

RJ opened a cabinet door. Inside was a varied display of knives. She bypassed all the biggest, sharpest and deadliest of knives, her hand coming to rest on a what appeared to be a parachute cord bracelet with a metal clasp.

"This is something they might not take from you. You can wear it around your wrist or ankle." RJ touched a button on the side of the metal clasp and the clasp opened, revealing a short, sharp knife.

Kinsley wrapped the bracelet around her wrist and played with it several times, making sure she knew how to easily open it.

"JoJo should be here by now. We should get ready to head out."

Kinsley's heart sputtered then raced ahead. She wasn't trained in combat. Her skills were in healing, not hurting. But, with her brother's life in the balance, she'd do whatever she had to. She just wished she could see Sawyer one more time.

He'd become her rock in an uncertain climate. And he'd touched her in ways she'd never felt before. Both physically and emotionally. If she came through this challenge alive, she wanted to spend more time getting to know the Navy SEAL. Already, her heart knew what her mind wasn't quite ready to accept.

CHAPTER 10

"I COUNT four guards scattered round the perimeter," Sawyer reported into his headset.

"We've got four on the road, alone," Jake said, his voice clear in Sawyer's ear. Hank had spent the money to get only the best communications devices.

"Are the gate guards in a black pickup with a machine gun mounted on the back?" Sawyer asked.

"Affirmative," Jake replied.

"Any sign of Derek Brothers or Bradshaw?" Cage Weaver asked. The man had arrived at the ranch at four o'clock that morning when the men had agreed to meet.

In less than an hour, they'd briefed Cage, collected the gear they would need and loaded four-wheelers onto a trailer hitched to a four-wheel drive one-ton pickup.

They'd trailered the four-wheelers as far as they

could and had found a place to park the truck and trailer in a stand of trees off the road near a flat area. By the time the sky had started to lighten, they'd been mounted on the ATVs and headed up old mining trails they'd located on the contour maps.

The trails got them to within a mile of the compound. At the designated point, they'd hidden the ATVs in the brush and continued on foot, climbing steep terrain to a ridge that overlooked The Collective's compound two hundred yards below.

Also on that ridge they'd discovered a single guard armed with an expert sniper rifle with a scope that could pinpoint a target over four hundred yards away.

Fortunately, that guard had been asleep and hadn't woken up enough to hear Max sneak up on him.

Max had been able to subdue him, clap a piece of duct tape over his mouth and secure him with zip-ties. To make double sure the man didn't alert the others, he'd tied him to a tree. He'd taken the man's radio from him and clipped it to his own belt.

Sawyer carried a rifle slung across his armored vest, a handgun tucked into a holster at his side and a knife clipped to his belt. He almost felt like he had when he'd been on active duty, fighting the Taliban or Al-Qaeda in Africa. With one exception. He didn't have use of his left forearm. Which made it difficult to handle a rifle. But he could.

He'd practiced on a range in Maryland using a rifle, shooting one-handed from the hip, rather than holding it up to his shoulder. He'd gotten pretty good at it. But not as accurate as he'd been when he'd been able to hold it with both hands. But he could manage, and that was what counted.

"Everyone have a good vantage point?" Jake asked.

All three men responded affirmative.

"Now, we wait," Jake said.

Sawyer raised a small set of binoculars to his eyes and studied the compound that consisted of what appeared to be an old mining ghost town.

The closer he looked, the more he realized the weathered buildings had been reinforced with new lumber and solid doors. What had once been houses for the miners and their families had deteriorated, until recently. Now they were storage and living quarters for The Collective. On a rise above the group of houses stood a larger building that had once been the entrance to a working mine, possibly where they'd processed the ore to extract the gold. Several trucks and vans stood outside the structure.

As light filled the sky, people emerged from the buildings, moving around with purpose, as if preparing for something.

A dozen men carried large white plastic bags filled with something, moving them from the old mine to the waiting vans and stacking them inside.

Other men carried metal ammo boxes, loading

them into the beds of the trucks, along with rifles, grenade launchers and more.

"You see what I'm seeing?" Max murmured.

"Looks like they're getting ready to supply an army with enough weapons and ammo to fight a full-scale war," Jake said.

"Or, like Swede said, are they loading up to move to another location?" Sawyer suggested.

"It could be, but what's in those white bags they're loading into that van?" Cage's voice chimed in. "That worries me the most. Guns and ammo are a known threat."

"Could they be loading..." Jake cursed. "Fertilizer. They're loading fertilizer into those vans."

"What the hell?" Max muttered. "That's enough fertilizer to treat a whole lot of fields."

"Or blow up a whole lot of building," Jake said. "They're planning something."

"We can't let them follow through on their plan," Weaver said. "The last time fertilizer was used as a bomb was that explosion in Oklahoma City where all those kids were killed and injured in that daycare. This can't be happening. Not here in Colorado."

"What better place?" Sawyer commented. "With the mountains and old mines to hide their activities, they've been able to stockpile fertilizer sufficient to blow a hole in Pikes Peak."

"We have to do something," Weaver said.

"Not until we get Derek Brothers out of there,"

Sawyer said. "The kid can't be mixed up in any plot to blow up shit. If he thinks he can't get away from this group now, he won't be able to shake its legacy if they end up killing someone."

"Hey," Jake interrupted. "The guy who just came out of the biggest miner's house, is that Bradshaw, aka Blade?"

Sawyer trained his binoculars on the man dressed in black jeans and a black T-shirt. He walked alongside a younger man, who was a little taller than he was but painfully thin compared to the leader of The Collective.

Bradshaw reached out and popped the younger man upside his head.

The younger man stopped in his tracks and refused to follow the older one.

Bradshaw turned and spoke angrily to the guy, shaking his fist at him. The younger dude squared his shoulders, lifted his chin and said something Sawyer couldn't make out by sound or lip reading.

Bradshaw marched toward him and slapped him hard across the cheek.

The younger man reeled backward, pressing a hand to a cut on his cheekbone. He dropped his hand, lifted his chin again and stood toe to toe with the group's leader, refusing to back down.

Again, Bradshaw slapped his face, the sound like a loud crack Sawyer could hear it all the way up to the top of the ridge.

"Why doesn't the kid punch the snot out of Bradshaw?" Jake spoke angrily.

"I'm betting that's Quillen Bradshaw taking a beating from his loving father," Sawyer said. "The waitress at the diner in town was dating that boy. Daddy wasn't too happy."

"Daddy doesn't look too happy about much," Cage said. "Makes me want to go down there and give the old man a taste of his own medicine."

"Get in line," Sawyer said. "That's no way to treat your kid."

"Or anyone else, for that matter," Jake added.

"Amy said Quillen and Derek had been seen together in town a couple days before we showed up." Through the binoculars, Sawyer watched as the father and son came to a stop in front of the old mine building.

If Quillen had befriended Derek Brothers, Derek couldn't be too far away.

Marion Bradshaw spoke to one of the men holding a rifle, standing beside the vehicles.

The man nodded, stepped back and waited while Bradshaw climbed into the front passenger seat of one of the empty vans that hadn't been filled with the bags of fertilizer.

A large man, who could have moonlighted as a bar bouncer, slipped behind the steering wheel. Several other men entered the van through a sliding side door. They all wore jackets over their T-shirts.

As it was still warm and summertime, the jackets didn't make sense. However, if they had guns hidden beneath those jackets, it made perfect sense to wear a jacket in the middle of the summer.

A wary chill slithered down Sawyer's spine and made him want to rip back those jackets and expose whatever they might be hiding beneath them.

The young man Bradshaw had been slapping around stood beside the van, his chin still jutting high. His father and the vanload of Collective members left the group of buildings and headed down the road to the gate where Sawyer and Kinsley had been denied entrance to the compound.

"Where do you think Bradshaw's going?" Jake asked.

"Don't know and don't care," Sawyer said. "All I do know is that now might be a good time to get in, find Derek and leave before their leader returns."

"Too many men milling around, loading those trucks," Weaver spoke softly. "They'll see us before we have a chance to pull someone aside to question the whereabouts of Kinsley's brother."

"There might not be a good enough time to make our move," Sawyer insisted. Now that they were there and Bradshaw was gone, he was ready to get in and get out with Kinsley's brother.

"What's happening down there isn't looking good. If they're planning to blow something up soon, they won't want to leave anyone who might name those responsible. And they won't drag anyone to their next location who doesn't back their cause."

"Good point."

"Check out the kid," Max said, his voice tight.

Sawyer watched as the man holding the rifle stepped forward and hit Bradshaw's kid with the butt of his weapon.

Quillen slumped to the ground.

The man with rifle motioned for two men to carry the younger man into the mine building.

"Wow. Bradshaw is a piece of work," Sawyer said. "If he's willing to have his men clock his own son, what has he done to Kinsley's brother?"

KINSLEY LEFT her rental SUV parked in the visitor parking lot at the east end of the Fool's Gold ghost town and walked slowly down the cobblestone street, feeling as if she were walking into a trap.

Hell, it was a trap. But what choice did she have? If she didn't show up, there was no telling what they'd do to Derek. At least, if they were going to use her to lure Sawyer out of the woods, that might give her the time to get herself free, find Derek and get away from Marion Bradshaw and his nutcase fanatics.

"You still with us?" RJ said into Kinsley's ear, making her jump slightly.

Without moving her lips, she responded. "Still

here." She couldn't have Bradshaw or his guys guessing that she was wired with a radio headset. They might assume she was working with the police and make a run for it.

Her gaze scanned the false store fronts, hoping to see her brother. The saloon was the second to the last building at the west end of the ghost town. Several people wandered the street, taking pictures of each other in front of different buildings, smiling and laughing. Without a care in the world. They didn't know a life-or-death situation was playing out in front of them like a shootout in an old western movie.

Kinsley hoped they didn't get caught in the crossfire. If there were any shots fired. Hopefully, that wouldn't happen. Still, she wasn't sure how they'd take her.

At gunpoint?

Tossed over someone's shoulder and thrown into a trunk?

Drugged and carried out by some of Blade's henchmen?

Whatever happened, she prayed they thought nothing of the bracelet she'd secured around her wrist or the necklace she'd worn since Sawyer had given it to her. When the guys did get back in range of a cell tower, their phones would be bombarded by RJ's, JoJo's and Kinsley's texts, giving them brief snippets of what was going down and when.

Since her own cellphone hadn't rung yet, she could only assume the men were still high on the mountain, spying on Bradshaw and members of The Collective.

Only some of Bradshaw's people wouldn't even be on that mountain. Bradshaw himself might not be there, if he planned to orchestrate Kinsley's kidnapping.

She hoped he would be there in Fool's Gold. That way, if the guys made their move while he was gone, they wouldn't have to deal with the man's terrible temper.

Kinsley was stuck with that lovely task.

As she arrived in front of the saloon, she stood with her shoulders back, her head held high and her stomach knotted.

"Going in," she murmured, hoping her mic picked up her words.

"Good luck," RJ said. "We're with you in spirit, if not in body."

"Thanks," Kinsley said. It was nice to know she had someone at her back, even if they couldn't do anything to help her. This was something Kinsley had to do on her own. She really hoped they took her to where they were holding Derek.

As she stepped up to the swinging doors, two men materialized from the sides of the building and closed in behind her.

Out of the corner of her eye, she could see the

dark metal of the handguns each carried, pointed at her.

"I take it you two men are my escort?" she said out loud. She pushed through the swinging doors and stepped into the saloon. Her eyes took a moment to adjust from the bright sunlight outside to the dingy darkness inside.

A man sat the bar, tapping his fingernails on the wooden counter.

When she could make out more than just his silhouette, she sighed. "Mr. Bradshaw."

"Ms. Brothers. Seems like we saw each other recently."

"And we did." She tilted her head toward the two men flanking her. "You must think I'm dangerous to send two hulking men out to move me along."

Bradshaw shrugged. "I didn't know whether you'd bring reinforcements. I didn't want to take any chances. Especially since I'm on a tight deadline. You've already caused enough trouble."

Kinsley hiked an eyebrow. "Trouble? All I've done since I've been here is to visit friends and look around at what Colorado has to offer."

"And drive up a road you and your man had no business driving on."

"From what I've seen of the road, it's not all that. Seems pretty heavily guarded for a farming community." She raised an eyebrow and propped a fist on one hip. "What are you hiding up there?"

"None of your business." His eyes narrowed. "Question is...why did you lie to the sheriff about looking for a man who owes you money instead of telling him the truth—that you were looking for your brother?

She met his gaze. "None of your business."

He smirked. "Touché."

"So, why did you want me to meet you here?"

His mouth curved into a tight smile. "I owe your man for what went down in the diner yesterday."

Kinsley snorted. "I knew it. Your ego couldn't take that kind of hit without wanting to give a little back."

Bradshaw's mouth twisted into an unattractive line. "Yeah, and by having you in my back pocket, your boy won't bail before we make our mark."

"Mark?" Kinsley cocked a single eyebrow.

The leader of The Collective's mouth spread into a grin that made Kinsley's skin crawl. "I guess you'll have to wait and see."

Kinsley lifted her chin. "Where's Derek?"

"Safe," Bradshaw replied.

"I told you I would leave if you didn't bring my brother." She backed a step and turned.

The two men who'd escorted her into the saloon, blocked her path.

"And I told you I'd kill him if you didn't show up." Bradshaw's voice was low and intimidating. "Now, I suggest you come with me or I'll give the word to dump your brother in a deep mine shaft where he'll die of his injuries or starve to death before anybody finds him."

Kinsley's belly clenched. "You wouldn't do that."

"No? Are you willing to bet Derek's life on that hunch?"

Kinsley didn't know how far she could push Bradshaw. She suspected he took great pleasure in scaring people.

She looked down her nose at the bastard, wanting so badly to punch him in the throat. "So, what happens next?"

"You're going to get into the van behind this building, and we're going back to the compound."

"And my brother?"

"Might live to see another day. I haven't decided. I guess it all depends on you and your boyfriend."

"I don't have a boyfriend," she insisted.

"You were pretty tight with the man you were with at the diner yesterday. The man who stepped over the line."

"He stepped over the line?" Kinsley snorted. "You were the one being a jackass."

Bradshaw's hand moved so fast Kinsley didn't have a chance to duck or block the blow that slammed into the side of her head.

She staggered backward and swayed, her vision blurring with the pain shooting across her temple.

"I don't have much patience for name-calling."

Kinsley pressed her hand to the side of her face

and felt something wet. She pulled her hand away only to find blood on her fingertips.

She stared at the man's fingers. He wore a large, metal ring around his middle finger. It must have cut her face.

Blood dripped down the side of her face. Kinsley pressed the palm of her hand to the source of the bleeding and held firmly to stop the flow. "From what I've observed, you don't have patience for much of anything."

"If you keep that in mind, you might not get hurt again." Bradshaw turned and led the way to the back of the saloon where a door stood open to the outside.

The two men who'd blocked her escape guided her to the exit, giving her little nudges to keep her moving when she wanted to run and hide.

"I guess I'm going with him," she said, not so much for her escorts but for the two women who were on the other end of her communications devices.

When they didn't respond, Kinsley thought maybe they were afraid Bradshaw and his creepy men would overhear the sounds and discover she'd not come alone as he'd demanded.

A man stood beside the van. As they approached, he turned and slid open the door.

Kinsley gasped.

On the floor, with their mouths gagged, their

wrists zip-tied behind their backs and their ankles secured as well, lay RJ and JoJo.

Kinsley received a shove from behind that sent her flying into the van, where she landed on top of RJ and JoJo.

The two men who'd shoved her climbed in behind her and held her down while they secured her wrists and ankles much like RJ's and JoJo's. At least, they didn't gag her.

Kinsley clamped down hard on her tongue to keep from cursing out loud. If she made a sound, it would remind them that they hadn't done anything to keep her from screaming or calling out for help. Not that she would.

She wanted to be taken to wherever they kept prisoners. Derek would be there, and then they'd figure a way out of the mess they'd landed in.

CHAPTER 11

SAWYER INCHED CLOSER to the compound, now only a few yards from the nearest old house with the gray, weathered exterior boards.

To someone just glancing toward the structures, they'd assume they were old and falling down.

Sawyer stood close enough he could see the plywood someone had hung inside to ward off the chilly night air and to keep the old boards from falling down. Someone had put time and money into shoring up the old mining town.

A man emerged from the building, carrying a backpack and a gym bag. Others carried their personal belongings in suitcases or large trash bags, tossing them into the backs of the trucks.

The flow of bags of fertilizer had come to a halt when the backs of the vans were full.

Sawyer wanted to run forward and slash the tires

on all of those vans to keep them from leaving the compound.

But he knew that would only slow them down for a short amount of time. They had to come up with a way to keep The Collective from blowing up a government building or something else equally tragic.

He and his team had taken their time moving down the side of the hill, barely finding enough vegetation to conceal their efforts. All it would take was for someone to look up, and they'd be swarmed.

With only four of them from the Brotherhood Protectors and fifty or sixty of The Collective, they faced over ten-to-one odds. Sawyer and the other members of the team were highly skilled at combat, but that was always the last option when no other resolution could be found. Their best bet would be to sneak in, liberate Derek and get the heck out with none being wise to their mission.

The trouble was, they weren't sure where Derek was being held.

"I'm going into this one," Sawyer said.

"Go easy. You don't want to alert the entire camp," Jake warned.

"Roger." Sawyer kept to the shadows, moving alongside the opposite side of the building from where the men were loading the pickups and vans.

As he reached the corner, he peered around,

waiting for a moment when all attention was on the vehicles, not the old houses.

Then he made his move. Walking like he was any other member of The Collective, he strode to the door, pushed it open and walked right in like he owned it. They'd purposely dressed in dark clothes like Bradshaw so they could blend into the shadows as well as with the men in the camp. Even The Collective's body armor was black. Thankfully, the Brotherhood Protectors had the choice of black for night operations and camouflage.

A quick look around, using the light coming through the cracks in the wall boards, revealed this particular house hadn't been shored up as well as others. Sawyer was careful where he stepped because the floorboards were rotting in many places. He left the building moments later and walked to the next one. No one stopped him or questioned who he was.

They were so busy loading available vehicles, with items from the old mine, they weren't paying attention to the man going through the other buildings.

Sawyer made it through the second building without incident. He was on the way to the third house when a van raced up the gravel road toward him.

He ducked into the shadows and watched as the van came to a halt beside the old mine

Men leaped out, and Bradshaw dropped from the passenger seat onto the ground.

Three of the men who'd gotten out of the van reached back in one at a time. The first man came out with the body of a woman slung over his shoulder like a sack of potatoes. She was small with dark brown hair. Her wrists and ankles had been bound, and she had a piece of duct tape over her mouth.

The man carried her into the mine.

"Guys, I don't know if you're seeing this…" Sawyer said. "They just carried a woman into the mine."

The second man came out of the van with another woman also bound in zip-ties and duct tape. She had sandy-blond hair and was much taller than the other woman and vaguely familiar, except for the tape over her mouth.

When the third man straightened from the van, Sawyer felt as if someone had sucker-punched him in the gut.

The woman the man carried had dark auburn hair. He only knew one woman with that color hair. "They have Kinsley," he whispered into his mic. "And if I'm not mistaken, RJ. The other woman was petite with long dark hair."

Max swore and growled. "They have JoJo."

"Hold steady," Jake said. "We're pretty much outnumbered. If we go charging in, we'll do no one any good if we're mowed down in the process."

"But they have JoJo," Max said, his voice tight as if he were talking through clenched teeth.

Sawyer could relate. He hated standing back when Kinsley was being carried into an abandoned mine. Those men might kill her and leave her in some deep shaft never to be recovered.

"Bullshit," Sawyer murmured. "They can't get away with this."

"Stand down, Sawyer," Jake ordered. "My woman is in there as well. We can't do anything that jeopardizes their lives."

"True, but we can't stand around doing nothing."

"We need backup," Jake said. "I need to get somewhere we can get reception so that I can contact Hank. If he can't get here soon enough, he might know people who can."

"In the meantime, they're carrying our ladies into that mine," Sawyer said. "Anything could happen inside there."

"If we go rushing in, they might throw them down a shaft and leave them to die. Some of the vertical shafts go straight down for a hundred feet. A fall like that would kill them."

"Jesus, Jake," Max said into their ears. "We have to do something."

"We need a diversion," Jake said. "Max, do you still have some of that C-4?"

"I do," Max replied.

"Think you can get close enough to the front gate to get them excited?" Jake asked.

"I know I could for a chance to make some noise."

"Do it" Jake ordered. "Cage, cover for Max."

"Roger," Cage said.

"With the explosion, we'll draw them away from the mine so Sawyer and I can get inside."

"Give me five mikes, and I'll have that explosion you want," Max said.

For the next few minutes, Sawyer counted the beats of his heart. He moved back out to the perimeter and worked his way around the site to get closer to the mine building.

"Sawyer, you in place by the old mine?" Jake asked.

Sawyer studied the distance and the obstacles in his way of the mine entrance. "I'm in place. I can be through the door in under two seconds."

"Same," Jake said.

Moments later, an explosion rocked the compound, and a cloud of dust rose up from the direction of the gate, providing concealment

People streamed out of the mine building and the other houses that had been nothing more than skeletons made of rotting boards when The Collective took control.

Sawyer pulled a black baseball cap out of the cargo pocket on the side of his pants and pulled it way down on his forehead. In the confusion of everyone rushing to see what had happened, Sawyer and Jake slipped into the mine building.

WHEN THE MAN carried Kinsley into the old mine, she willed him to hurry and put her down. The sooner she could get the knife out of her bracelet, the sooner she'd be able to free RJ and JoJo.

Not to mention...they were inside The Collective's compound. Somewhere close, her brother was alive, waiting for Kinsley to find him. All she needed was for the big oaf carrying her to *Put. Her. Down.*

The lighting in the mine building was dim, but she could see enough from hanging upside down to know they'd been using it as a storage facility for lots of things, including guns, ammunition, grenades, bags of fertilizer and rocket launchers. She might not be up on current laws, but weren't rocket launchers illegal for civilians to own?

Her heart beat faster. These people weren't preppers waiting for an EMP to take down the electric grid. They were staging enough weapons and ammunition to wage a war.

But against whom?

Bradshaw followed the man carrying Kinsley through the mine building to where the man stopped.

"Put her with the others down below."

The man grunted his acknowledgement and

dumped Kinsley on a metal floor in what appeared to be a metal cage. She landed beside JoJo and RJ. The man stepped in with the women and punched a red button.

The cage lurched, and then descended slowly down a long, narrow shaft, the dingy yellow light at the top of the elevator car reflecting off the rock walls on the outside of the cage.

"Where are you taking us?" she asked softly, still afraid he'd slap duct tape over her mouth, but more afraid of how deep they were descending into the bowels of the earth.

"To where no one will hear or find you," he said in a coarse, gravelly voice that sounded like he chewed on nails for fun.

The deeper they went, the more alarmed she grew. They would be left at the bottom of a vertical mineshaft. Their escort would take the elevator back to the top, leaving them to die below.

Kinsley studied the shiny walls of the shaft. There had to be a way out other than the elevator. If the elevator broke down, the miners had to be able to get themselves to the surface.

The walls in front of her were bare and slick. She twisted around, until she could see the wall behind her. A rusty metal ladder was attached to the rock wall, leading all the way to the surface. As long as it went all the way to the bottom, they might have a chance.

When the elevator finally touched ground at the bottom of the shaft, the man with them stepped out into another mine shaft stretching out in front of them. The light from the elevator car barely illuminated the car. It didn't shed much more light on the shaft leading away.

The man moved the women by grabbing an arm or a leg and dragging them off the metal floor onto the cool rock floor of the shaft.

Once they were all out, he stepped back into the car.

"You can't leave us here to die," Kinsley said. "That's murder."

The man stared through her, not at her, as he punched the red button inside the rudimentary elevator. The cage shuttered and rose up the shaft, taking what little light it provided with them.

The farther up the shaft it went, the darker it became where Kinsley lay against the cold floor.

She didn't wait for the elevator to disappear out of sight before she worked her fingers around the clasp on the bracelet they had left on her wrist. With a soft snick, the clasp released, and the bracelet fell to the ground.

Kinsley felt around for the braided parachute chord, careful not to cut her fingers on the blade she'd freed from its casing. Once she had it in her hands, she worked the blade against the plastic zip-tie.

The light disappeared altogether, leaving her working her bindings behind her back and completely blind.

"I'm going to get us out of this," she said quietly.

JoJo and RJ tried to respond, but the duct tape over their mouths kept their words at a mumble. Another sound caught Kinsley's attention from a little further away than where the women were dumped. She paused. "Hello?"

A sound similar to that of JoJo and RJ's pitiful attempts to speak came to Kinsley in the darkness. "Is someone else down here with us? Grunt once for yes."

A grunt sounded. A moment later, another grunt sounded. There were at least two more people in the shaft with them.

"As soon as I get through my zip-tie, I'll help everyone else. Hang on." She sawed at the plastic, her efforts hampered by the fact she only had her fingertips to work with. Still, she worked at the bindings until, finally, the plastic broke.

Kinsley immediately went to work on the ties around her ankles, quickly sawing through them. Then she felt her way in the dark along the floor until she found one of the women. She wasn't sure which one. It didn't matter.

She had her zip-ties cut in less than a minute.

As soon as the woman's hands were free, Kinsley went to work on the ties around her ankles. A moment later, a sticky, scraping sound was followed by the woman breathing a relieved sigh. "Holy hell," RJ said. "They make removing tape from your face look easy in them movies. I think I lost a full layer of skin. What can I do to help?"

"There are others with us. Find them while I free JoJo," Kinsley said.

She patted the ground, moving in the direction she remembered the other woman had been left.

Soon, JoJo was free.

"Ouch, ouch, ouch," she said as she eased the tape off her face. "Bastards!"

"Did you find them?" Kinsley called out to RJ.

"Yes. Follow my voice," RJ said. "I'll keep talking until you make it over to me. There are two others over here. Men, by the deep sounds of their grunts."

Kinsley crawled across the floor toward RJ's voice. When she found the woman's leg, RJ grasped her hand and guided it to the zip-tie around a man's wrists.

Kinsley used the knife to break through the plastic then cut the tie around his ankle.

"Oh, thank God," a gravelly voice croaked. "I thought we'd die down here."

RJ found her arm and guided her to the next man. Soon, she had his hands free. She was working on his ankles when he was finally able to speak.

"Kinsley?" a familiar voice sounded in her ear.

Her heart leaped, and a sob rose up in her throat. "Derek?"

"Oh, dear God, Kinsley."

Arms wrapped around her, crushing her to her brother's chest. "Derek. What the hell?" she said, her voice cracking.

"I'm sorry," he said. "I'm so sorry I got you into this mess."

"You didn't know, sweetie. You didn't know what he would do." She leaned back and adjusted the bracelet knife in her hand. "Let me get your ankles loose."

As she cut at the zip-tie, her brother rested his hand on her back.

"I didn't realize what they were planning until I got up here. I hired on to work in construction. They said it was a summer job, that they'd pay me well. When I got here...sweet Jesus, they're crazy. They wanted me to join them in some crazy-ass plan to take over the Colorado capital and declare Colorado a country of its own." Derek laughed, the sound raw and humorless. "Hell, we have to get out of here. We have to warn the police, the national guard...anyone who'll listen. They have enough stuff to blow Denver off the map. So many people will be killed. It'll be Oklahoma City all over again...only worse."

"We can't do anything from down here," the other guy said into the dark, his voice that of a young man. His voice came from behind Kinsley. "There's a button somewhere on the wall the miners used to call the elevator back to the bottom."

"Who are you?" RJ asked, her voice floating in the black abyss. "I mean, I figure one of you guys is Kinsley's brother and all. But I'd like to know who the other one is."

A soft snort sounded in the inky black. "I'm the enemy."

"Somehow, I don't believe that." RJ said. "If you were the enemy, you wouldn't be in this hell hole with us."

"I'm worse than the enemy, I'm the son of the bastard who has completely lost his mind and is planning to launch a coup against the Colorado government."

"You're Quillen Bradshaw," Kinsley said.

"Don't listen to him," Derek said. "He's not the enemy. He just had lousy luck picking parents."

"Look, *muchacho*," JoJo said. "I don't care who your parents are. What I care about is this… If we get out of this shaft, will you stand with us or turn on us?"

"I tried to talk him out of this," Quillen said. "It's a suicide mission, not to mention, it'll hurt so many innocent people." He paused. "I'd do anything to stop this from happening. I'd stand with you." He shuffled around more and stopped. "Here. The button's here." A metal clang echoed against the walls of the shaft.

Kinsley held her breath, waiting to hear the sound

of the elevator on its way down the shaft. And she waited.

Nothing.

Quillen hit it again.

Again, nothing.

"They turned off the power," Quillen said.

"You mean we're stuck down here?" RJ asked. "Don't some of these shafts lead out of the mountain?"

"Not anymore," Quillen said. "The ones that lead out have been closed."

"What do you mean closed?" JoJo asked. "Like doors and locks?"

"No," Quillen said. "Like using dynamite to seal the entrances."

"Great," RJ laughed. "And the only people who know where we are will be heading to Denver to blow shit up. They're not going to stop along the way and confess to trapping five people at the bottom of some random mineshaft. We could use some heroes about now."

"Right?" JoJo snorted. "Where are our men?"

"The irony is that they're out there," RJ said. "Not too far away."

"They'll never hear us down here. I mean, listen to this... Hey!" JoJo shouted at the top of her lungs. The sound echoed against the walls of the shaft. The elevator didn't magically descend, no one shouted back.

"We're too far down," Derek said quietly.

If she could escape the mine any other way, Kinsley would have, but the way she saw it, there was only one way out. "Guys, there's a ladder that goes to the top."

"You realize how far up that is?" RJ asked.

"And you're not big on heights, are you Sis?" Derek slipped his arm around Kinsley's shoulder. "If you'd like, I'll follow you up, just in case you slip."

She leaned into him. "When did you grow up and become a man?"

"When I had to. About the time Blade Bradshaw told us he'd kill anyone who tried to leave. This was his way of passively killing me. He left me here, knowing I couldn't get free of the zip-ties and that I'd starve to death at the bottom of this shaft."

"That's even more cruel than putting a bullet through your head," JoJo said.

"Tell me about it," Derek said. "I'd already been down here for a day when they brought Q down—and now you three."

"Well, we're not staying down here," Kinsley squared her shoulders and raised her hands in front of her, feeling for the walls of the shaft and the ladder that was their ticket to freedom.

Her fear of heights took second billing to her fear of dying of starvation in a mine. She wanted to see the light again, to smell something besides damp rocks. And she wanted to make love with Sawyer.

When her hands bumped into metal rungs, her heart turned over and her breathing became more difficult.

She drew in a slow, steady breath. Now was not the time to hyperventilate. "I'm going up. You can follow or wait for me to send help down."

"I'm not staying down here another second," Derek said. "Besides, I promised I'd follow you up."

"I don't know how old this ladder is, or how sturdy," Kinsley said.

"Maybe we should spread out so we don't put too much weight on any one section," RJ said. "Do you want me to go first?"

Kinsley shook her head then realized no one could see the movement. She almost laughed at herself. "No. I'll go." She gripped the rung above her head, placed her foot on the bottom rung and pulled herself up.

"One foot at a time," Derek whispered.

And that was what she did. One rung at a time, she moved up the ladder.

"Imagine you're only three feet off the ground. It's so dark in here, you'd never know the difference."

Kinsley laughed. "I'm okay. It really does help that I can't see the bottom."

"Good. And I'm here if you slip." Derek touched her heel. "I've never been so glad to hear your voice as I was a few minutes ago."

"And I'm glad we found you. Now, I'm going to

conserve my lung power so I can make it all the way to the top. We'll talk when we're out of here."

Kinsley had never climbed a ladder out of a mine-shaft. She hoped she had the strength to reach the top. There was no going back. Not with the others on their way up behind her.

She didn't want to think about what they might face at the top. Bradshaw's people might still be in the mine building. What then?

One step at a time. She'd cross that bridge when she reached the top of the shaft.

CHAPTER 12

THE LIGHTING in the old mine building was so bad, the men moving about, loading equipment and ammunition, didn't notice the two men wearing baseball caps as they slipped through the door and into the shadows. Even carrying weapons, they blended in with the members of The Collective who were armed to the teeth.

"Can you see where they took the women?" Sawyer asked.

"No," Jake said. "There are too many people in the way. I don't even see the guys who carried them in."

"We have to find them." Sawyer worried that Bradshaw would take out his anger on them. That he'd brought them to his compound meant one thing. He wanted Sawyer to pay for embarrassing him at the Cripple Creek diner.

It showed what a narcissist the man was that he'd

go to all the trouble of capturing Kinsley and the other women to pay him back. Especially when he was staging some operation. His people were working frantically to get everything in the trucks and vans. His ego had taken a huge hit. Why else would he slow the works to seek revenge?

The crowd of people thinned as many of them grabbed something and headed out the door.

That was when Sawyer spotted Bradshaw standing beside the large man who'd carried Kinsley into the building.

Bradshaw nodded and turned his attention to the masses of people who were carrying stuff out to the waiting vehicles. "Time's up," he yelled out loud. "Load what you have and forget the rest. I want you all on the road ASAP."

The scurrying became more frenetic as people hurried with their burdens out the door.

As the room cleared, Sawyer and Jake had no more luck locating Kinsley, JoJo and RJ.

"Where did they take them?" Sawyer whispered.

"I don't know," Jake said. "But we better find them before Bradshaw leaves. If they took them into the mineshafts, we might never find them in the maze of tunnels."

"You guys, the gate is blown wide open, and all those vehicles are headed our way," Cage reported. "There's enough debris on the ground to slow them down, but not for long."

"We can't let them get to any major towns or cities," Jake said. "Not with what they're carrying."

"There's only four of us, and a whole lot more of them," Max said.

"Make that twelve," another voice sounded in Sawyer's ear. Who had come on their frequency?

"That you, Hank?" Jake chuckled. "How'd you hear about our little party?"

"Got word from Swede. I was just landing at the Fool's Gold airport when I got the texts that Kinsley was meeting with Bradshaw."

"Apparently, she did," Jake confirmed. "And so did RJ and JoJo. He's got all three of them somewhere in the mine building in his compound. How many of the brotherhood do you have with you?"

"Eight, counting me. We're dropping in as we speak."

"Dropping?" Jake grinned. "Chutes or lines?"

"Chutes," Hank said. "Will be on the ground in two mikes. And we have the local law enforcement and state police on their way."

"Whatever you do, don't let the convoy of vehicles get down off the mountain. They're loaded with enough stuff to take out a good portion of Denver.

"Roger. See you in a few. Let's wrap this up and make it back to the ranch for supper."

"Yes, sir," Jake said quietly.

Jake stared across at Sawyer. "You heard the man. Let's wrap this up."

All the while Jake had been talking softly to the man in his ear, Sawyer had his eye on Bradshaw. The man knew where the women were.

"I'm going for Bradshaw," he said.

"You won't get close enough. He's got half a dozen men around him."

"I don't care. He knows where they are." Sawyer moved through the building, slipping through the shadows, closing the distance between himself and the leader of The Collective. As he passed a large support beam, a blinking light caught his attention. He paused and stared at a small clock with numbers ticking downward. Five minutes and fifty-four seconds. He glanced around at the other beams in the building. On some, he could see other blinking lights. More C4, more detonators set on a timer.

His stomach knotted and the blood rushed from his head. "Guys," he said into his mic. "We've got a problem We have less than nine minutes until this building lights up like the Fourth of July.

"Explain,"

"Someone's wired this building with explosives. From the bomb next to me, we have nine minutes and twenty-seven seconds left to clear the building before it comes down on anything and anyone left inside."

"Have you found JoJo?" Max asked.

"Not yet," Jake responded.

"Don't leave that building without her," Max said.

"I wouldn't dream of it," Jake assured him quietly.

Sawyer pulled the timed detonator out of the lump of pliable plastic explosives, dropped it on the ground and ground it beneath his boot. It was only one. How many more were in the building? And where were Kinsley, JoJo and RJ?

He set his watch to reflect the amount of time they had left to clear the building. It wasn't much.

While Sawyer shifted his attention to the explosives, Bradshaw moved from where he'd been standing, heading for the exit.

"Everybody out," Bradshaw called out. "T-minus seven and counting. If you're not out in nine minutes, you're dead."

Make that eight minutes and thirty seconds.

A man walked up to Bradshaw, leaned toward him and said something in his leader's ear.

Bradshaw nodded and peered into the shadows, squinting. Then he drew back his head and shouted, "Sawyer Johnson. We've been waiting for you and the rest of your friends. You might as well come on out. You won't get out of this building unless you do. My men are waiting at the exits."

"I'm going," Sawyer said into his mic.

"I've got your six," Jake answered.

With little time to spare, Sawyer stepped out into the open. "Bradshaw, where are they?"

The man turned toward Sawyer and sneered. "Not so funny when you're the one on the spot, is it?"

"This isn't about being on the spot. It's about three women who've done nothing to you and who won't make it out of this building alive unless you tell me where you're holding them." Sawyer took a step closer, holding out the gun in his hand so Bradshaw would know he meant business. "Where are they?"

Bradshaw backed away a step, his eyes widening. "You won't shoot me, because I'm the only one who can tell you where they are. If I'm dead, you'll never find them. And don't forget, you're outnumbered. All I have to do is say the word and any one of my men will shoot you dead." He inched toward the big guy standing beside him, using the man's body as a shield.

Sawyer held up his watch. "You have eight minutes. If they aren't leaving, neither are you."

"You can't keep me here," he said. "I'll have my men shoot you first."

"Try me." Sawyer glared at the man.

His bodyguard raised his weapon, aiming at Sawyer's chest.

Sawyer raised his weapon but didn't have to fire.

A shot rang out from behind him.

Jake.

The bullet hit the big man in his dominant arm. The man yelped, dropped his weapon and grabbed his arm.

"Did you know your boss has this place wired to explode in less than seven minutes?"

The man shook his head.

Sawyer aimed a glare at the big man. "Are you going to die with him when he wasn't going to tell anyone the building was coming down? Consider this...he's hiding behind you. You might be willing to take a bullet for him, but would he take one for you?"

The big man glanced back at Bradshaw once, and then holding his injured arm, he ran for the exit, shouting to others to do the same. "The building's going to explode. Get out!"

Without his guy in front of him, Bradshaw stood exposed, a pistol in his hand, aimed at Sawyer. "Want to play a little game of chicken?"

"I'm tired of playing games." Sawyer fired, hitting Bradshaw in the chest.

Bradshaw staggered backward, dropping his gun in the process. "You won't find them," he said and collapsed to his knees. "Save yourself...or don't." He lay on the ground, his hand clutching the wound on his chest. He was still breathing, but every breath gurgled.

Sawyer didn't give him another thought. He rushed past him, shouting, "Kinsley, RJ, JoJo!"

Jake joined him, shouting as loudly as Sawyer.

They raced to the back of the building where a cage hovered over the top of a shaft. Voices sounded as if far away.

The closer they came to the shaft, the louder the voices until one stood out above the rest. Sawyer's heart squeezed tightly in his chest. "Kinsley!"

"Sawyer?"

The cage was one that took miners down a vertical shaft. Sawyer circled the cage and found nothing behind it. No rooms, no people.

"Sawyer! We're down here," Kinsley called out.

"Where?" He tried to look down the shaft through the cage, but the floor of the cage was a solid sheet of metal, and the shaft was as dark as pitch.

"In the mine shaft," Kinsley answered. "Coming up the ladder."

Sawyer glanced at his watch. Five minutes and fifteen seconds. He circled again, locating the ladder at the back of the shaft. There was only enough room for a person to squeeze between the elevator car and the wall of the mineshaft.

"Do you have RJ and JoJo with you?" Jake called out.

"We're here," RJ shouted from further below.

"And we have two more," Kinsley added. "Derek and Quillen. Almost there."

Sawyer pulled a small flashlight from one of his pockets and shined it down the ladder. The beam glinted off Kinsley's auburn hair. She pulled herself up the ladder one rung at a time, as if she was exhausted.

"Sweetheart, you all need to make it up here as fast as you can. Bradshaw set explosives throughout the building. They're due to go off in," he glanced at his watch, "Four minutes and fifty-four seconds."

Her eyes widened, and she renewed her efforts to get to the top as quickly as possible. When she was within reach, Jake leaned hard against the elevator cage, shoving it as far over as it would go.

Sawyer grabbed Kinsley's hand with his and pulled her out of the shaft, setting her on her feet.

Kinsley immediately turned back to help Sawyer pull her brother out next.

"RJ?" Jake called out.

"Jake, I'm coming as fast as I can."

Sawyer shined his light down at her. She was only seven rungs from the top. "I'll lean on the cage."

Jake nodded and reached for RJ. When her hand landed in his, he yanked her up through the gap. She scrambled out of the way and helped him pull JoJo out.

"Need to hurry it up," Sawyer said as he leaned against the cage. "We only have two more minutes and forty-five seconds. We still need to get out of the building."

Derek and Jake reached for Quillen's hands and dragged him through the gap. As he lurched to his feet, they all turned as one. The race to leave the building was a race for their lives.

"Follow me," Quillen said. "I know the way."

He led them through the maze of old rusted equipment and broken boards, aiming for the light streaming through the open door at the other end of the long building.

Only halfway there Quillen ground to an abrupt halt.

Sawyer almost plowed into him. They had less than two minutes remaining. When Sawyer looked over the young man's shoulder, he saw why he'd stopped.

Lying on the ground, holding a handgun in his grip, was Marion Bradshaw.

"You never were worth the money I spent to feed and clothe you," Bradshaw said, his words gurgling, blood dripping from the corner of his mouth.

"You never were the father I deserved," Quillen said. "I couldn't be like you. You're mean. You beat my mother. She was smart to leave you. I only wish she'd taken me with her."

The older Bradshaw snorted and coughed up blood. "She didn't leave you. She's at the bottom of that mine shaft where you were supposed to die with her."

"Bastard!" Quillen lunged at his father, kicking at the gun in his hand. A shot rang out before the gun flew across the ground.

Quillen clutched at his side but remained standing. "I hope you rot in hell." Then he staggered away from his father.

"One minute, twenty seconds," Sawyer called out. "Run!" He pushed Kinsley ahead of him, looped Quillen's arm over his shoulder and ran with him toward the door.

Jake came up on Quillen's other side. Between the two of them, they got Quillen through the door and out into the open air and sunshine.

"Don't stop!" Sawyer yelled.

Kinsley had slowed, but turned again and ran alongside RJ and JoJo.

Derek turned back and took Sawyer's place.

They'd cleared twenty yards between them and the building when a series of explosions rocked the earth.

"Get down!" Jake yelled.

They all fell to the ground.

Sawyer covered Kinsley's body with his as the building behind them erupted, showering boards, tin, rocks and debris all around them.

For a long moment, Sawyer lay with his body protecting Kinsley's. When he was fairly sure the last bit of explosives had been spent, he rolled off her and pushed to his feet. His ears rang and his back would be bruised, but they were alive.

He held out his hand and pulled Kinsley to her feet.

She flung her arms around his neck and clung to him.

Sawyer circled her back, holding her close, loving the feel of her body pressed to his. "I could do this all day...and night," he whispered against her ear.

Kinsley leaned back and stared up into his eyes, her own filling with tears. "When I was at the bottom of that shaft, all I could think was that I wanted to see you again. On the climb up in the dark, I thought about how you made me feel safe when we looked over the edge of that cliff. You held me close then, and the memory held me close on the climb up."

"You had me worried," he admitted. "With the clock ticking away, I wasn't sure we'd find you in time."

"How did that make you feel?" she asked. "I know how I felt when I thought I might not see you again." She paused, and then stared up into his eyes. "Heartbroken."

"That's how I felt. I was desperate to find you. I wasn't going to leave that building without you."

Her brow furrowed, and she reached up to touch his cheek. "Had you stayed, you would have died."

"Failure wasn't an option," he insisted and bent to claim her lips. This was where he belonged. With this woman, holding her and kissing her like there was no tomorrow. There had almost been no tomorrow for them. Once again, he'd been given a second chance.

He wouldn't squander it feeling sorry for himself. He had worth and purpose. If nothing else, he'd been spared twice now so that he could protect Kinsley.

"I never believed in fate, until I met you," he said.

She smiled up at him. "And now you do?"

He nodded. "I believe fate brought us together on that plane, and fate stirred up that storm to keep us together."

Kinsley wrapped her arms around his waist and pressed her cheek against his armored vest. "She's tricky, that Fate."

"You two done sucking face?" Jake called out from ahead of them on the road toward the gate.

Rotating lights blinked red and blue as DEA agents, state police and the local sheriff's department surrounded the men driving the trucks and vans full of everything needed to start a big fight with the government.

Jake and Sawyer were joined by eight strange men, Sheriff Parker, Max and Cage. They met on the gravel road and shook hands.

Jake pulled one of the men toward him. "Sawyer, this is the man who started the Brotherhood Protectors, Hank Patterson."

Sawyer took the man's hand. "We know each other."

Hank nodded and pulled Sawyer into a hard hug. "Yes, we do. I was thrilled when you accepted the position with Jake here in Colorado. We need good men like you, Jake, Cage and Max to build this division up like we did in Montana." He stepped back and grinned. "And just two days into the job, and you've already knocked out your first assignment."

"It took the team," Sawyer said, glancing around at his new team, his heart swelling at the feeling of belonging and purpose.

"How did you get here so quickly from California?" Jake asked.

Hank grinned. "Actually, I was on my way out before all this blew up. There's a five-man team of Green Berets who just came off active duty. We're interviewing them in a week. I wanted to be here to greet them and assure them we want the kind of skills they bring to the table."

Jake nodded. "Good. We could've used them today rather than rely on flying your guys in from Montana."

"Are you kidding? These guys were beside themselves to have a chance to drop in by parachute. I had to scramble a sky-diving plane out of Colorado Springs that was about to take off with paying customers. They landed on the strip outside Fools' Gold, equipped us with chutes and gave us a great ride."

"And thank goodness they landed when then did," Max said. "The Collective had the rubble cleared from the gate and were just getting back into their vehicles when Hank and his guys strode up the road. Less than a minute later, the DEA, ATF and state police showed up." Max turned to the sheriff.

Sheriff Parker nodded. "We'd been working in conjunction with the DEA and ATF to collect the evidence we needed about an attempt to overthrow the government."

Jake waved toward the trucks and vans lined up

on the gravel road. The men who'd been driving them sat on the ground, their wrists bound, awaiting transport to jail. "Think you'll have enough evidence now?"

The sheriff nodded. "They've assured me they do. And you helped us avert a terrible attack on our population. Thank you."

Sawyer pulled Kinsley close. "I'm just glad we got these people out of the mine in time."

"Me, too," Jake smiled down at RJ and pressed a kiss to her forehead. "I've gotten used to having you around."

"Same," she said and stood on her toes to press her lips to his in a brief kiss.

"Can I give your people a ride back to town?" Sheriff Parker asked.

"We need to collect our ATVs," Jake said. "But the rest of these people need transportation back to Lost Valley Ranch."

"We can make that happen." Sheriff Parker tipped his head toward Quillen. "Thank you for assisting our investigation. We couldn't have done it without your help."

Quillen's lips pressed into a tight line. "I couldn't let them do it."

"It can't have been easy to go against your father," Jake said.

"Easier than you think." Quillen glanced back at the destroyed building where his father lay entombed. "He was a hard man to live with. But he's gone now. Buried in an explosion of his own doing."

Sheriff Parker laid a hand on the young man's shoulder. "I'd like you to come with me to the station."

"Sure," he said. "I also have information on the whereabouts of my mother. Apparently, my father killed her and ditched her body in the mine."

The sheriff shook his head. "At least we can close that missing persons case and lay your mother to rest."

Kinsley hugged Sawyer around the waist. "I want to stay with you."

"And I'd rather you stayed with me. But it's rough country, and we only have enough room in the truck for the four of us. I'll see you back at the lodge."

Kinsley nodded. She joined JoJo, RJ, Quillen and Derek and walked past the prisoners and down the road to where the sheriff waited with his full-sized SUV.

"I've never been more scared in my life." Jake stood beside Sawyer, his gaze on RJ as they climbed into the sheriff's vehicle.

"Me, too," Max said. "The thought of losing JoJo nearly broke me."

Sawyer nodded. He'd felt the same about Kinsley. "How long do you have to know someone before you know she's the one?"

"A day," Jake answered.

"A moment," Max offered and clapped a hand on Sawyer's shoulder. "Kinsley's amazing. Don't let her get away."

Sawyer would do his best to woo her and make her want to stay. He knew in his heart she was amazing and the one for him. He'd spend the rest of his life convincing her, if that's what it took.

EPILOGUE

One week later

SAWYER SAT on the porch swing with Kinsley, gently rocking back and forth. The afternoon sun hovered over the peaks and slipped below the ridge line, plunging the porch and its occupants into the gentle gray of dusk.

Kinsley leaned her head against his shoulder, a smile curving her lips.

Sawyer loved that look of contentment.

Derek sat on the steps, whittling a hawthorn branch.

Gunny had given him the knife and showed him how to use it without cutting himself. He said it was good therapy to keep his hands busy and his mind off the trauma of being trapped by The Collective at the bottom of a black abyss of a mine shaft.

Kinsley had notified her parents of their son's drama and assured them he was okay and safely staying at the Lost Valley Ranch until he could enroll in college the next semester. After playing at the ski resorts and his run-in with the anarchists, he was ready to do something useful with his life. He was even considering joining Army ROTC. One day, he hoped to join the Special Forces, having been inspired by the men of the Brotherhood Protectors.

Hank had stayed for the week, working with Jake, going over names of Special Forces operatives who'd recently separated from their branches of service. Hank wanted to grow the Colorado division of the Brotherhood Protectors.

"I've invited five former members of 10th Special Forces to join us at the Watering Hole tomorrow afternoon. Kujo will be flying into Colorado Springs tomorrow around noon. I'll pick him up and bring him out."

Hank handed out a sheet of paper to each member of the team. "This is an abbreviated list of the men, their ranks, experience and skills."

"Why are you interviewing all five at once," Jake asked.

"They've operated as a team and are very close-knit. I suspect if I hire one, I'll have to hire all five."

"What's their story?" Max asked. "Why are they all separating from the Army?"

Hank's eyes narrowed. "I got information from one of my inside contacts that they were involved in a mission gone wrong. Their commander gave a bad order, and then let them take the fall for him."

"He threw them under the bus?" Cage shook his head. "That's bad form." He glanced up from the paper he held in his hand. "They appear to be highly qualified and decorated. They deserve a second chance."

Hank nodded. "I hope to give it to them. Thing is, they're still smarting from the blackeye the Army gave them. They were given the choice of leaving or being court martialed."

"That's not much of a choice," Sawyer said.

"No, it isn't." Hank held out the paper. "But these guys were career Army. They loved what they did and took pride in doing it well. I want them on the team, if they want to join us."

Cage grinned from where he leaned against the porch rail, his fiancée, Emily Strayhorn beside him. "Are you telling us to act nice?"

Hank chuckled. "No. I want you to be yourselves. I value each one of you and your opinions. If you don't think they'll fit, I expect you to let me know." He turned to Sawyer. "As the newest member of the team, you can tell them what it's like starting out with us."

Sawyer laughed. "Do you want me to tell them the truth or a lie?"

Hank grinned. "Always the truth."

"It's a wild ride," Sawyer said. "But I'd do it all again." He squeezed Kinsley's hand. "I've met some amazing people in the process. And I've found a place I think I can call home."

"Lost Valley Ranch?" Gunny asked.

"Colorado," Sawyer clarified, and then in a tone only Kinsley could hear he added, "with you."

She leaned closer, resting her head on his shoulder. "I don't work for the Brotherhood Protectors, but I can say the same. I'd do it all again." Her eyebrows dipped. "Except maybe the climb up the mine shaft." She laughed. "My muscles are just now recovering. And I've signed up with a personal trainer in Fool's Gold to improve my upper body strength, just in case I ever get into a similar situation. Not that I plan on it. I'll keep my feet on the surface from now on."

RJ and JoJo laughed.

"Agreed," RJ said.

"And I got a job," Kinsley said.

"Where?" RJ asked.

"At the hospital in Fool's Gold. I also found an apartment. We—I'll be moving in next week." She blushed a pretty shade of pink.

Kinsley had asked Sawyer if he wanted to move into the two-bedroom apartment with her.

He'd wanted to jump at the chance, but insisted they date for a few more weeks to make sure that was what she really wanted. He didn't want to rush her into something she wasn't sure about, although he was absolutely sure about her.

He couldn't imagine himself with anyone else. But he planned to visit her often and take her out as many times as she could stand.

"I love spending time with you, Kinsley Brothers," he whispered.

"Then move in with me," she whispered back.

"I would in a heartbeat."

"But?" she cocked an eyebrow.

"But I want *you* to be sure. I come with baggage." He tipped his head toward his left arm.

"That's just plain bullshit," she said. "You're perfect, and I love you for exactly who you are. There...I said the 'L' word." She lifted her chin. "I have no regrets, and I won't take it back. In fact, I'll say it louder so that everyone can hear."

She turned to the others on the porch. "Even though I've only known him for a week and a couple days, I love this guy. He's everything I could ever want in a man and more." She faced him, her eyes glowing with her emotion. "Sawyer, you're my hero in every way, and I don't care if the entire world knows. But if you need time to learn to love me... well then, hurry up. I'm ready to start our forever together."

He laughed and gathered her close. "You're a mess, Kinsley, and I love that about you. And if it's forever you're after…you've come to the right place."

She sighed and leaned into him with a smile. "I've come home.

BREAKING SILENCE

DELTA FORCE STRONG BOOK #1

New York Times & USA Today
Bestselling Author

BREAKING
Silence

New York Times & USA Today Bestselling Author

ELLE JAMES

CHAPTER 1

HAD he known they would be deployed so soon after their last short mission to El Salvador, Rucker Sloan wouldn't have bought that dirt bike from his friend Duff. Now, it would sit there for months before he actually got to take it out to the track.

The team had been given forty-eight hours to pack their shit, take care of business and get onto the C130 that would transport them to Afghanistan.

Now, boots on the ground, duffel bags stowed in their assigned quarters behind the wire, they were ready to take on any mission the powers that be saw fit to assign.

What he wanted most that morning, after being awake for the past thirty-six hours, was a cup of strong, black coffee.

The rest of his team had hit the sack as soon as they got in. Rucker had already met with their commanding officer, gotten a brief introduction to the regional issues and had been told to get some rest. They'd be operational within the next forty-eight hours.

Too wound up to sleep, Rucker followed a stream of people he hoped were heading for the chow hall. He should be able to get coffee there.

On the way, he passed a sand volleyball court where two teams played against each other. One of the teams had four players, the other only three. The four-person squad slammed a ball to the ground on the other side of the net. The only female player ran after it as it rolled toward Rucker.

He stopped the ball with his foot and picked it up.

The woman was tall, slender, blond-haired and blue-eyed. She wore an Army PT uniform of shorts and an Army T-shirt with her hair secured back from her face in a ponytail seated on the crown of her head.

Without makeup, and sporting a sheen of perspiration, she was sexy as hell, and the men on both teams knew it.

They groaned when Rucker handed her the ball. He'd robbed them of watching the female soldier bending over to retrieve the runaway.

She took the ball and frowned. "Do you play?"

"I have," he answered.

"We could use a fourth." She lifted her chin in challenge.

Tired from being awake for the past thirty-six hours, Rucker opened his mouth to say *hell no*. But he made the mistake of looking into her sky-blue eyes and instead said, "I'm in."

What the hell was he thinking?

Well, hadn't he been wound up from too many hours sitting in transit? What he needed was a little physical activity to relax his mind and muscles. At least, that's what he told himself in the split-second it took to step into the sandbox and serve up a heaping helping of whoop-ass.

He served six times before the team playing opposite finally returned one. In between each serve, his side gave him high-fives, all members except one— the blonde with the blue eyes he stood behind, admiring the length of her legs beneath her black Army PT shorts.

Twenty minutes later, Rucker's team won the match. The teams broke up and scattered to get showers or breakfast in the chow hall.

"Can I buy you a cup of coffee?" the pretty blonde asked.

"Only if you tell me your name." He twisted his lips into a wry grin. "I'd like to know who delivered those wicked spikes."

She held out her hand. "Nora Michaels," she said.

He gripped her hand in his, pleased to feel firm pressure. Women might be the weaker sex, but he didn't like a dead fish handshake from males or females. Firm and confident was what he preferred. Like her ass in those shorts.

She cocked an eyebrow. "And you are?"

He'd been so intent thinking about her legs and ass, he'd forgotten to introduce himself. "Rucker Sloan. Just got in less than an hour ago."

"Then you could probably use a tour guide to the nearest coffee."

He nodded. "Running on fumes here. Good coffee will help."

"I don't know about good, but it's coffee and it's fresh." She released his hand and fell in step beside him, heading in the direction of some of the others from their volleyball game.

"As long as it's strong and black, I'll be happy."

She laughed. "And awake for the next twenty-four hours."

"Spoken from experience?" he asked, casting a glance in her direction.

She nodded. "I work nights in the medical facility. It can be really boring and hard to stay awake when we don't have any patients to look after." She held up her hands. "Not that I want any of our boys injured and in need of our care."

"But it does get boring," he guessed.

"It makes for a long deployment." She held out her hand. "Nice to meet you, Rucker. Is Rucker a call sign or your real name?"

He grinned. "Real name. That was the only thing

my father gave me before he cut out and left my mother and me to make it on our own."

"Your mother raised you, and you still joined the Army?" She raised an eyebrow. "Most mothers don't want their boys to go off to war."

"It was that or join a gang and end up dead in a gutter," he said. "She couldn't afford to send me to college. I was headed down the gang path when she gave me the ultimatum. Join and get the GI-Bill, or she would cut me off and I'd be out in the streets. To her, it was the only way to get me out of L.A. and to have the potential to go to college someday."

She smiled "And you stayed in the military."

He nodded. "I found a brotherhood that was better than any gang membership in LA. For now, I take college classes online. It was my mother's dream for me to graduate college. She never went, and she wanted so much more for me than the streets of L.A.. When my gig is up with the Army, if I haven't finished my degree, I'll go to college fulltime."

"And major in what?" Nora asked.

"Business management. I'm going to own my own security service. I want to put my combat skills to use helping people who need dedicated and specialized protection."

Nora nodded. "Sounds like a good plan."

"I know the protection side of things. I need to learn the business side and business law. Life will be different on the civilian side."

"True."

"How about you? What made you sign up?" he asked.

She shrugged. "I wanted to put my nursing degree to good use and help our men and women in uniform. This is my first assignment after training."

"Drinking from the firehose?" Rucker stopped in front of the door to the mess hall.

She nodded. "Yes. But it's the best baptism under fire medical personnel can get. I'll be a better nurse for it when I return to the States."

"How much longer do you have to go?" he asked, hoping that she'd say she'd be there as long as he was. In his case, he never knew how long their deployments would last. One week, one month, six months…

She gave him a lopsided smile. "I ship out in a week."

"That's too bad." He opened the door for her. "I just got here. That doesn't give us much time to get to know each other."

"That's just as well." Nora stepped through the door. "I don't want to be accused of fraternizing. I'm too close to going back to spoil my record."

Rucker chuckled. "Playing volleyball and sharing a table while drinking coffee won't get you written up. I like the way you play. I'm curious to know where you learned to spike like that."

"I guess that's reasonable. Coffee first." She led him into the chow hall.

The smells of food and coffee made Rucker's mouth water.

He grabbed a tray and loaded his plate with eggs, toast and pancakes drenched in syrup. Last, he stopped at the coffee urn and filled his cup with freshly brewed black coffee.

When he looked around, he found Nora seated at one of the tables, holding a mug in her hands, a small plate with cottage cheese and peaches on it.

He strode over to her. "Mind if I join you?"

"As long as you don't hit on me," she said with cocked eyebrows.

"You say that as if you've been hit on before."

She nodded and sipped her steaming brew. "I lost count how many times in the first week I was here."

"Shows they have good taste in women and, unfortunately, limited manners."

"And you're better?" she asked, a smile twitching the corners of her lips.

"I'm not hitting on you. You can tell me to leave, and I'll be out of this chair so fast, you won't have time to enunciate the V."

She stared straight into his eyes, canted her head to one side and said, "Leave."

In the middle of cutting into one of his pancakes, Rucker dropped his knife and fork on the tray, shot out of his chair and left with his tray, sloshing coffee as he moved. He hoped she was just testing him. If she wasn't…oh, well. He was used to eating meals alone. If she was, she'd have to come to him.

He took a seat at the next table, his back to her, and resumed cutting into his pancake.

Nora didn't utter a word behind him.

Oh, well. He popped a bite of syrupy sweet pancake in his mouth and chewed thoughtfully. She was only there for another week. Man, she had a nice ass…and those legs… He sighed and bent over his plate to stab his fork into a sausage link.

"This chair taken?" a soft, female voice sounded in front of him.

He looked up to see the pretty blond nurse standing there with her tray in her hands, a crooked smile on her face.

He lifted his chin in silent acknowledgement.

She laid her tray on the table and settled onto the chair. "I didn't think you'd do it."

"Fair enough. You don't know me," he said.

"I know that you joined the Army to get out of street life. That your mother raised you after your father skipped out, that you're working toward a business degree and that your name is Rucker." She sipped her coffee.

He nodded, secretly pleased she'd remembered all that. Maybe there was hope for getting to know the pretty nurse before she redeployed to the States. And who knew? They might run into each other on the other side of the pond.

Still, he couldn't show too much interest, or he'd be no better than the other guys who'd hit on her. "Since you're redeploying back to the States in a week, and I'm due to go out on a mission, probably within the next twenty-four to forty-eight hours, I don't know if it's worth our time to get to know each other any more than we already have."

She nodded. "I guess that's why I want to sit with you. You're not a danger to my perfect record of no fraternizing. I don't have to worry that you'll fall in love with me in such a short amount of time." She winked.

He chuckled. "As I'm sure half of this base has fallen in love with you since you've been here."

She shrugged. "I don't know if it's love, but it's damned annoying."

"How so?"

She rolled her eyes toward the ceiling. "I get flowers left on my door every day."

"And that's annoying? I'm sure it's not easy coming up with flowers out here in the desert." He set down his fork and took up his coffee mug. "I think it's sweet." He held back a smile. Well, almost.

"They're hand-drawn on notepad paper and left on the door of my quarters and on the door to the shower tent." She shook her head. "It's kind of creepy and stalkerish."

Rucker nodded. "I see your point. The guys should at least have tried their hands at origami flowers, since the real things are scarce around here."

Nora smiled. "I'm not worried about the pictures, but the line for sick call is ridiculous."

"How so?"

"So many of the guys come up with the lamest excuses to come in and hit on me. I asked to work the nightshift to avoid sick call altogether."

"You have a fan group." He smiled. "Has the adoration gone to your head?"

She snorted softly. "No."

"You didn't get this kind of reaction back in the States?"

"I haven't been on active duty for long. I only decided to join the Army after my mother passed away. I was her fulltime nurse for a couple years as she went through stage four breast cancer. We thought she might make it." Her shoulders sagged. "But she didn't."

"I'm sorry to hear that. My mother meant a lot to me, as well. I sent money home every month after I enlisted and kept sending it up until the day she died suddenly of an aneurysm."

"I'm so sorry about your mother's passing," Nora said, shaking her head. "Wow. As an enlisted man, how did you make enough to send some home?"

"I ate in the chow hall and lived on post. I didn't

party or spend money on civilian clothes or booze. Mom needed it. I gave it to her."

"You were a good son to her," Nora said.

His chest tightened. "She died of an aneurysm a couple of weeks before she was due to move to Texas where I'd purchased a house for her."

"Wow. And, let me guess, you blame yourself for not getting her to Texas sooner...?" Her gaze captured his.

Her words hit home, and he winced. "Yeah. I should've done it sooner."

"Can't bring people back with regrets." Nora stared into her coffee cup. "I learned that. The only thing I could do was move forward and get on with living. I wanted to get away from Milwaukee and the home I'd shared with my mother. Not knowing where else to go, I wandered past a realtor's office and stepped into a recruiter's office. I had my nursing degree, they wanted and needed nurses on active duty. I signed up, they put me through some officer training and here I am." She held her arms out.

"Playing volleyball in Afghanistan, working on your tan during the day and helping soldiers at night." Rucker gave her a brief smile. "I, for one, appreciate what you're doing for our guys and gals."

"I do the best I can," she said softly. "I just wish I could do more. I'd rather stay here than redeploy back to the States, but they're afraid if they keep us here too long, we'll burn out or get PTSD."

"One week, huh?"

She nodded. "One week."

"In my field, one week to redeploy back to the States is a dangerous time. Anything can happen and usually does."

"Yeah, but you guys are on the frontlines, if not behind enemy lines. I'm back here. What could happen?"

Rucker flinched. "Oh, sweetheart, you didn't just say that…" He glanced around, hoping no one heard her tempt fate with those dreaded words *What could happen?*

Nora grinned. "You're not superstitious, are you?"

"In what we do, we can't afford not to be," he said, tossing salt over his shoulder.

"I'll be fine," she said in a reassuring, nurse's voice.

"Stop," he said, holding up his hand. "You're only digging the hole deeper." He tossed more salt over his other shoulder.

Nora laughed.

"Don't laugh." He handed her the saltshaker. "Do it."

"I'm not tossing salt over my shoulder. Someone has to clean the mess hall."

Rucker leaned close and shook salt over her shoulder. "I don't know if it counts if someone else throws salt over your shoulder, but I figure you now need every bit of luck you can get."

"You're a fighter but afraid of a little bad luck."

Nora shook her head. "Those two things don't seem to go together."

"You'd be surprised how easily my guys are freaked by the littlest things."

"And you," she reminded him.

"You asking *what could happen?* isn't a little thing. That's in-your-face tempting fate." Rucker was laying it on thick to keep her grinning, but deep down, he believed what he was saying. And it didn't make a difference the amount of education he had or the statistics that predicted outcomes. His gut told him she'd just tempted fate with her statement. Maybe he was overthinking things. Now, he was worried she wouldn't make it back to the States alive.

* * *

NORA LIKED RUCKER. He was the first guy who'd walked away without an argument since she'd arrived at the base in Afghanistan. He'd meant what he'd said and proved it. His dark brown hair and deep green eyes, coupled with broad shoulders and a narrow waist, made him even more attractive. Not all the men were in as good a shape as Rucker. And he seemed to have a very determined attitude.

She hadn't known what to expect when she'd deployed. Being the center of attention of almost every single male on the base hadn't been one of her expectations. She'd only ever considered herself average in the looks department. But when the men outnumbered women by more than ten to one, she guessed average appearance moved up in the ranks.

"Where did you learn to play volleyball?" Rucker asked, changing the subject of her leaving and her flippant comment about what could happen in one week.

"I was on the volleyball team in high school. It got me a scholarship to a small university in my home state of Minnesota, where I got my Bachelor of Science degree in Nursing."

"It takes someone special to be a nurse," he stated. "Is that what you always wanted to be?"

She shook her head. "I wanted to be a firefighter when I was in high school."

"What made you change your mind?"

She stared down at the coffee growing cold in her mug. "My mother was diagnosed with cancer when I was a senior in high school. I wanted to help but felt like I didn't know enough to be of assistance." She looked up. "She made it through chemo and radiation treatments and still came to all of my volleyball games. I thought she was in the clear."

"She wasn't?" Rucker asked, his tone low and gentle.

"She didn't tell me any different. When I got the scholarship, I told her I wanted to stay close to home to be with her. She insisted I go and play volleyball for the university. I was pretty good and played for the first two years I was there. I quit the team in my third year to start the nursing program. I didn't know there was anything wrong back home. I called every week to talk to Mom. She never let on that she was sick." She forced a smile. "But you don't want my sob story. You probably want to know what's going on around here."

He set his mug on the table. "If we were alone in a coffee bar back in the States, I'd reach across the table and take your hand."

"Oh, please. Don't do that." She looked around the mess hall, half expecting someone might have over-heard Rucker's comment. "You're enlisted. I'm an officer. That would get us into a whole lot of trouble."

"Yeah, but we're also two human beings. I wouldn't be human if I didn't feel empathy for you and want to provide comfort."

She set her coffee cup on the table and laid her hands in her lap. "I'll be satisfied with the thought. Thank you."

"Doesn't seem like enough. When did you find out your mother was sick?"

She swallowed the sadness that welled in her throat every time she remembered coming home to find out her mother had been keeping her illness from her. "It wasn't until I went home for Christmas in my senior year that I realized she'd been lying to me for a while." She laughed in lieu of sobbing. "I don't care who they are, old people don't always tell the truth."

"How long had she been keeping her sickness from you?"

"She'd known the cancer had returned halfway through my junior year. I hadn't gone home that summer because I'd been working hard to get my coursework and clinical hours in the nursing program. When I went home at Christmas..." Nora gulped. "She wasn't the same person. She'd lost so much weight and looked twenty years older."

"Did you stay home that last semester?" Rucker asked.

"Mom insisted I go back to school and finish what I'd started. Like your mother, she hadn't gone to college. She wanted her only child to graduate. She was afraid that if I stayed home to take care of her, I wouldn't finish my nursing degree."

"I heard from a buddy of mine that those programs can be hard to get into," he said. "I can see why she wouldn't want you to drop everything in your life to take care of her."

Nora gave him a watery smile. "That's what she said. As soon as my last final was over, I returned to my hometown. I became her nurse. She lasted another three months before she slipped away."

"That's when you joined the Army?"

She shook her head. "Dad was so heartbroken, I stayed a few months until he was feeling better. I got a job at a local emergency room. On weekends, my father and I worked on cleaning out the house and getting it ready to put on the market."

"Is your dad still alive?" Rucker asked.

Nora nodded. "He lives in Texas. He moved to a small house with a big backyard." She forced a smile. "He has a garden, and all the ladies in his retirement community think he's the cat's meow. He still misses Mom, but he's getting on with his life."

Rucker tilted his head. "When did you join the military?"

"When Dad sold the house and moved into his retirement community. I worried about him, but he's doing better."

"And you?"

"I miss her. But she'd whip my ass if I wallowed in self-pity for more than a moment. She was a strong woman and expected me to be the same."

Rucker grinned. "From what I've seen, you are."

Nora gave him a skeptical look. "You've only seen me playing volleyball. It's just a game." Not that she'd admit it, but she was a real softy when it came to caring for the sick and injured.

"If you're half as good at nursing, which I'm willing to bet you are, you're amazing." He started to reach across the table for her hand. Before he actually touched her, he grabbed the saltshaker and shook it over his cold breakfast.

"You just got in this morning?" Nora asked.

Rucker nodded.

"How long will you be here?" she asked.

"I don't know."

"What do you mean, you don't know? I thought when people were deployed, they were given a specific timeframe."

"Most people are. We're deployed where and when needed."

Nora frowned. "What are you? Some kind of special forces team?"

His lips pressed together. "Can't say."

She sat back. He was some kind of Special Forces. "Army, right?"

He nodded.

That would make him Delta Force. The elite of the elite. A very skilled soldier who undertook incredibly dangerous missions. She gulped and stopped herself from reaching across the table to take his hand. "Well, I hope all goes well while you and your team are here."

"Thanks."

A man hurried across the chow hall wearing shorts and an Army T-shirt. He headed directly toward their table.

Nora didn't recognize him. "Expecting some-one?" she asked Rucker, tipping her head toward the man.

Rucker turned, a frown pulling his eyebrows together. "Why the hell's Dash awake?"

Nora frowned. "Dash? Please tell me that's his callsign, not his real name."

Rucker laughed. "It should be his real name. He's first into the fight, and he's fast." Rucker stood and faced his teammate. "What's up?"

"CO wants us all in the Tactical Operations Center," Dash said. "On the double."

"Guess that's my cue to exit." Rucker turned to Nora. "I enjoyed our talk."

She nodded. "Me, too."

Dash grinned. "Tell you what...I'll stay and finish your conversation while you see what the commander wants."

Rucker hooked Dash's arm twisted it up behind his back, and gave him a shove toward the door. "You heard the CO, he wants all of us." Rucker winked at Nora. "I hope to see you on the volleyball court before you leave."

"Same. Good luck." Nora's gaze followed Rucker's broad shoulders and tight ass out of the chow hall. Too bad she'd only be there another week before she shipped out. She would've enjoyed more volleyball and coffee with the Delta Force operative.

He'd probably be on maneuvers that entire week.

She stacked her tray and coffee cup in the collection area and left the chow hall, heading for the building where she shared her quarters with Beth Drennan, a nurse she'd become friends with during their deployment together.

As close as they were, Nora didn't bring up her conversation with the Delta. With only a week left at the base, she probably wouldn't run into him again. Though she would like to see him again, she prayed he didn't end up in the hospital.

Breaking Silence

ABOUT THE AUTHOR

ELLE JAMES also writing as MYLA JACKSON is a *New York Times* and *USA Today* Bestselling author of books including cowboys, intrigues and paranormal adventures that keep her readers on the edges of their seats. When she's not at her computer, she's traveling, snow skiing, boating, or riding her ATV, dreaming up new stories. Learn more about Elle James at www.ellejames.com

Website | Facebook | Twitter | GoodReads | Newsletter | BookBub | Amazon

Or visit her alter ego Myla Jackson at mylajackson.com
Website | Facebook | Twitter | Newsletter

Follow Me!
www.ellejames.com
ellejamesauthor@gmail.com

Montana Rescue (Sleeper SEAL)

Hot SEAL Salty Dog (SEALs in Paradise)

Hot SEAL,Hawaiian Nights (SEALs in Paradise)

Hot SEAL Bachelor Party (SEALs in Paradise)

Hot SEAL, Independence Day (SEALs in Paradise)

Brotherhood Protectors Vol 1

The Outrider Series

Homicide at Whiskey Gulch (#1)

Hideout at Whiskey Gulch (#2)

Hellfire Series

Hellfire, Texas (#1)

Justice Burning (#2)

Smoldering Desire (#3)

Hellfire in High Heels (#4)

Playing With Fire (#5)

Up in Flames (#6)

Total Meltdown (#7)

Declan's Defenders

Marine Force Recon (#1)

Show of Force (#2)

Full Force (#3)

Driving Force (#4)

Tactical Force (#5)

Disruptive Force (#6)

Mission: Six

One Intrepid SEAL

Two Dauntless Hearts

Three Courageous Words

Four Relentless Days

Five Ways to Surrender

Six Minutes to Midnight

Hearts & Heroes Series

Wyatt's War (#1)

Mack's Witness (#2)

Ronin's Return (#3)

Sam's Surrender (#4)

Take No Prisoners Series

SEAL's Honor (#1)

SEAL'S Desire (#2)

SEAL's Embrace (#3)

SEAL's Obsession (#4)

SEAL's Proposal (#5)

SEAL's Seduction (#6)

SEAL'S Defiance (#7)

Hot Velocity (#4)

Cajun Magic Mystery Series

Voodoo on the Bayou (#1)

Voodoo for Two (#2)

Deja Voodoo (#3)

Cajun Magic Mysteries Books 1-3

SEAL Of My Own

Navy SEAL Survival

Navy SEAL Captive

Navy SEAL To Die For

Navy SEAL Six Pack

Devil's Shroud Series

Deadly Reckoning (#1)

Deadly Engagement (#2)

Deadly Liaisons (#3)

Deadly Allure (#4)

Deadly Obsession (#5)

Deadly Fall (#6)

Covert Cowboys Inc Series

Triggered (#1)

Taking Aim (#2)

Bodyguard Under Fire (#3)

Cowboy Resurrected (#4)

Navy SEAL Justice (#5)

Navy SEAL Newlywed (#6)

High Country Hideout (#7)

Clandestine Christmas (#8)

Thunder Horse Series

Hostage to Thunder Horse (#1)

Thunder Horse Heritage (#2)

Thunder Horse Redemption (#3)

Christmas at Thunder Horse Ranch (#4)

Demon Series

Hot Demon Nights (#1)

Demon's Embrace (#2)

Tempting the Demon (#3)

Lords of the Underworld

Witch's Initiation (#1)

Witch's Seduction (#2)

The Witch's Desire (#3)

Possessing the Witch (#4)

Stealth Operations Specialists (SOS)

Nick of Time

Alaskan Fantasy

Boys Behaving Badly Anthology

Rogues (#1)

Blue Collar (#2)

Pirates (#3)

Stranded (#4)

First Responder (#5)

Blown Away

Warrior's Conquest

Enslaved by the Viking Short Story

Conquests

Smokin' Hot Firemen

Protecting the Colton Bride

Protecting the Colton Bride & Colton's Cowboy Code

Heir to Murder

Secret Service Rescue

High Octane Heroes

Haunted

Engaged with the Boss

Cowboy Brigade

Time Raiders: The Whisper

Bundle of Trouble

Killer Body

Operation XOXO

An Unexpected Clue

Made in the USA
Las Vegas, NV
25 August 2021

28853881R00144